# Brothers in Blue and Red: Rescuing Ceili

By

## V. J. Devereaux

*As V. J. Devereaux*

***The Book of Demons series***
Demon's Kiss
Demon's Embrace

Cherry's Jubilee
Cooking Class

***The Bound Series***
Blood Bound
Magic Bound

Special Delivery

***The Brothers Series***
Brothers in Blue and Red: Saving Maya

*Discover other titles by Valerie Douglas*

**Fantasy**
*The Coming Storm Series*
The Coming Storm
A Convocation of Kings
Not Magic Enough
Setting Boundaries

*Song of the Fairy Queen*

*Servant of the Gods series*
Servant of the Gods
Heart of the Gods

**Romance**
*The Millersburg Quartet*
Irish Fling
Dirty Politics
Directors Cut
Two Up

**Romantic Suspense**
Lucky Charm

**Thrillers**
Nike's Wings
The Last Resort

*Dedication*


To Jolynn and Amanda, my lovely beta readers

Thanks, too, to the firefighters for information on fires, to Christopher with the Red Cross and Derek with SWAT for their advice


*Disclaimer*


Any and all errors in procedure for firefighters, paramedics, SWAT or the Red Cross are strictly the fault of the author.

Some of the characters in this book are based on real people and events. The names were changed to protect the guilty.

# Chapter One

A steady beeping, loud enough to be disturbing, woke Ceili out of a dead sleep. Her dog, Ranger, a Belgian Malinois, was whining and pawing at her bed. Ceili felt a little disoriented, oddly off. Her temples throbbed. She glanced up at the source of the sound. Her smoke detector – not the one provided by the apartment building management – was making the noise. Her bedroom seemed hazy as she glanced toward the window and the streetlight beyond it. She thought she smelled smoke. Not a lot, but there shouldn't be any.

Alarm shot through her.

"Ranger, out!" she said, reaching for her cell phone and dialing 911 even as she snatched up her robe. She ran toward the apartment door as she pulled the robe on.

Fumbling the door open, still half-asleep, she hurried to the main door into the building.

"Emergency, 911 what is your emergency?" a voice said.

She let Ranger out the front door, letting it shut, but not latch, behind her, otherwise the door would automatically lock until or unless the code was punched in. If it was only her imagination it was cold enough at that hour to not want to fumble at the door trying to get back in, especially wearing only a thin robe and nightgown.

"My name is Ceili Whelan, 2451 Collins Court. The smoke detector is going off in my apartment." She looked around. Her head was already clearing with the fresher air. No one else was outside. "I think there might be a leak of some kind or a fire in the building."

No lights were coming on in any of the other apartments but if she looked up, she could see a thin trickle of smoke rising above the building. That wasn't good. She shouldn't be seeing smoke there, but the smoke detector that was hard-wired to the building hadn't gone off either. It was an old system. Slightly greasy from cooking oil and dusty, she wasn't sure how well it worked, which was why she'd bought her own. Just in case.

It seemed as if 'just in case' had arrived.

She looked toward the basement windows. It was hard to tell if she was just seeing that someone had left the light on in the laundry area as they sometimes did or if it was something else. But she could definitely see a glow.

"Stay on the line, ma'am, the fire department is responding."

Looking up again, Ceili could see there were no lights on in the Johnson's apartment. They were home, she knew that since she'd passed Julie in the hall earlier. Both were also deaf. They wouldn't hear an alarm or sirens and their apartment and bedroom were at the back of the building so lights wouldn't disturb them either.

What she was going to do was stupid and she knew it. If there was a fire and the smoke detectors weren't going off, though, she had to wake them, get them out, though, and everyone else she could.

She started taking deep, long breaths. "Ranger, with me."

Opening the door quickly she let Ranger go ahead of her, then she quickly shut the door on her robe so the firefighters could get in, but fresh air wouldn't and fuel the fire.

Now she could see tendrils of smoke wisping from beneath the cellar door. She swore softly. Something *was* on fire in the basement. She wasn't opening that door or else give fresh fuel to the fire below.

To the 911 operator she said, "I see smoke coming from beneath the door to the basement."

It didn't seem like that much. She had time, she thought.

Holding her breath, she ran down the hall banging on the doors she passed.

"Fire," she shouted, as she hit the stairs to the second level.

It was almost as if she announced it.

Glass broke somewhere. Lots of it.

Suddenly from beneath the door to the basement storage area and laundry room a great gout of smoke erupted. More rolled past her, thick and black. How long had the fire been smoldering down there? She remembered all the boxes in the crawl space, the furniture piled against that wall, the kids' toys. She had researched causes of fires as part of her old job and all that junk stored in the basement had always given her the shudders. She had only moved in a few months before, so she'd hesitated to say anything.

All that junk stored down there…

Ceili raced up the stairs, shouting "Fire."

Below her she could hear doors opening and a couple panicked voices.

Smoke flowed from the air conditioning vents, rising toward the upper floors, joining the thick smoke billowing from below. How long had it been doing that? Was that why she'd felt so groggy when the alarm woke her? It was getting hard to see.

Hammering on doors as she went past, shouting "Fire", she kept running.

She hit the stairs to the third level staying low, scrambling up them.

The smoke was much thicker there, nearly impenetrable and so dark she could barely see her own hand in front of her face. She circled the rail, reached out to the find the wall, Ranger at her side.

Dropping to her hands and knees she crawled as quickly as she could toward where she thought the Johnsons' apartment was, feeling along the wall.

She heard sirens and she thought she saw the distant lights of fire engines flashing over the windows at the front of the building, barely cutting through the thick smoke.

Worse, though, was the smoke filling the building.

Banging and shouting, keeping as low as she could, she scrambled to the Johnson's apartment, but their emergency key was above the door. It was a stretch and a hop to get it down. She could no longer see for the smoke, but she scrabbled for it. The smoke was so thick now that the people coming out of their apartments were invisible.

Something in the basement roared. The fire had found more fuel or more air.

"Stay low," she shouted. "Go straight. Find the railing to the stairs. Hurry."

Unlocking the Johnson's door, she threw it open and Ranger raced through it. The air was slightly clearer there, but the smoke and the fumes that had set off her alarm had been rising through the vents for a while.

Dropping to her hands and knees again, Ceili followed Ranger as fast as she could.

Ranger barked. She followed the sound.

Both the Johnsons were still in bed.

"Ranger," she said, "Out!"

She hoped the firefighters would see him and guess someone up here had let him out.

The dog raced out of the apartment and down the stairs as Ceili shook Tony Johnson, hard.

He started, not quite awake, looking groggy. His breathing was wheezy when she leaned close, his eyes unfocused.

Ceili signed 'Fire' but he didn't respond. She went around the bed to Julie and shook her. Nothing. No response.

As far as Ceili could tell, both were breathing but Tony's sounded more like a wheeze. She could manage Julie, but Tony was just too big for her.

Knowing she didn't have much time before the smoke overcame her, too, she put her shoulder into him and rolled him off the bed into the slightly cleaner air by the floor. More gently, she did the same with Julie, cradling the woman's head.

She needed help.

Keeping low, she scrambled out of the apartment toward where she thought the stairs were. The smoke was so thick she couldn't see them. Below she heard Ranger barking and followed the sound. She found the stairs the hard way when she ran out of level floor, nearly pitching headfirst down, barely managing to turn around before she hit the landing. Sliding down on her butt seemed as expedient a way to get down the rest.

"Ranger," she shouted.

*****

The smoke was so thick Jesse couldn't see his own hand in front of his face. He wiped his mask again to try to clear it. He was astonished to hear a dog barking wildly at him and the other firefighters trying to evacuate the tenants from the building. It was close, but impossible to see in the smoke. The thermal imagining in his mask showed him that it was, indeed, a dog.

Then the dog was gone, running up, barking as it went

Signaling to his partner, Jesse turned on his hands and knees and went after it, maintaining his contact with the wall

to be sure he could find his way out again. He could feel
Mike's hand on his boot.

"There's a dog. Someone called it," he said over the
radio to Mike and the other firefighters on search and rescue
as he felt around for the stairs. "We've got someone up
above." Where the smoke was thickest.

To his surprise, someone was coming down the narrow
stairs by the most efficient manner possible if you were trying
to stay low. On their bottom. He found that out when a foot
clipped his shoulder.

He couldn't see them through the thick smoke.

"I've got someone," he said to Mike, as he caught
whoever it was around their legs, dragged them close.

Whoever it was jumped a little at his touch in surprise.

*****

With the thick smoke, Ceili's contact with the railing and
Ranger were her only way of knowing where she was. She
couldn't see a thing. She'd turned on the stair landing only
because it was slightly wider and her foot connected with the
opposite wall. Other than that, she was completely at a loss as
to how far away she was from the bottom of the stairs. She
was also coughing hard from the smoke.

She had a bad moment when someone clutched at her.
Vivid memories flashed through her mind before she realized
who it was more likely to be, a fireman, and relaxed.

A pair of hands clutched at her, dragged her down and
close.

"Ranger, out!" He couldn't be much better off than she
was.

She couldn't see the firemen at all.

Then they were at the door, two pairs of arms getting her
to her feet, and outside the building.

"Got her, Jesse?" the one said.

"Yeah, Mike, I got her."

*****

One of the other firefighters was feeding hose to those on the cellar stairs, others were pouring water through the cellar windows, trying to knock the fire down, as Jesse steered his victim toward the waiting emergency services vehicles, almost instinctively heading for his brother Justin.

For the first time, he got a look at his charge.

It was the brilliant golden-red hair reflected in the lights that caught his eye. The color was unusual, almost an amber. Her lightly freckled, fine-featured face was smoke-smudged, piercing blue eyes looked up at him in surprise. She was wearing nothing but a thin, very short cotton nightgown, which left little left to the imagination. He didn't need much imagination, either, the thin cotton revealed some very nice curves. Beneath the gown were shapely legs. She was barefoot, and something about those vulnerable naked feet caught at him.

A much besmudged robe to match her nightgown was just inside the main door. A lot of boots had tramped over it, but they hadn't had to break through the door to get inside. That had been quick thinking on her part and saved them from the time it would have taken to break through the heavy-duty combination lock – necessary in this part of town.

The dog stayed close, its eyes alert.

Fresher air roused her a bit, although she was coughing from the smoke. He set her down on the back bumper of his brother Justin's ambulance.

Now that he had, it was hard not to notice she was pretty beneath the smoke and soot, and that hair was remarkable. She also had nice curves, and truly excellent legs.

"Hey, Justin." He glanced at his brother, who was eyeing her appreciatively, too, before he turned professional paramedic again.

"What have you got Jess?" Justin asked, as he took the girl's pulse, watching her chest to check her breathing.

Brian, the EMT Justin was teamed with, was checking over the other survivors.

"Smoke inhalation."

Her hand lifted to rub between her eyebrows. "Considering some of what was down in the basement, it wasn't just smoke," she said, coughing. "It was my smoke detector that woke me, though. It went off, the building smoke alarms never did."

*****

Justin looped an oxygen tube beneath her nose, then over her ears, brushing her hair back to do so. That color was unique, a rich amber almost the color of the sunset. It was soft, too, smooth silky waves that fell to her collar and framed her pretty face. Her eyes were clear and brilliantly blue.

It took a breath to pull his mind back to checking her vitals. The rise and fall of her chest to check respiration was almost as distracting, given that her full breasts were barely hidden beneath the soft, thin, well-worn cotton of her nightgown, and the chill of the night was having a visible effect on them as well.

"What's your name?" Justin asked.

"Ceili Whelan," she said. "I called 911, but I knew the Johnson's were deaf and wouldn't hear sirens. Someone had to go help them. Both were still breathing, but I couldn't get them to answer me. I moved them down to the floor, but neither were responding. I couldn't carry either. I closed the door to keep any more smoke from entering their apartment, but left it unlocked and came to get help."

Jesse waved to the battalion chief.

"We've got two people upstairs, both deaf, neither are responding according to Miss Whelan. She's the one who called the fire in."

"Anyone else?" the Chief asked.

Ceili looked around. "Where are the kids? I don't see them. Have any kids been brought out?"

The Chief shook his head. "What apartment?"

"Second floor," she said. "The Monaghans. George and Marie, three kids in the back bedrooms. I babysit them, two boys and a girl."

"Jesse," the Chief said.

"On it," Jesse said. "Mike and I will take the third floor."

The Chief nodded, radioing a team to take a ladder around the back of the building.

"Wait," Ceili said, holding up her hands and wiggling her fingers. "This is the sign for fire. It looks like what it is."

He nodded, masking up again and calling Mike.

"Thank you, Miss Whelan," the Chief said. "You got her, Justin?"

He nodded, as the Chief and his brother strode away.

"How do you spell your name?" he asked. "K Y L I E?"

That pretty mouth curved a little into a wry smile. "No, my parents named me for the Irish dance and music party, so I'm literally named 'happy dance'." Her long-lashed blue eyes twinkled. "It's the hard Celtic C pronounced K, so C E I L I, although it should be pronounced Kayly, but no one ever does so I gave up trying.  Whelan with an A at the end. And you're Justin?"

He smiled in response. "Justin Armitage. Jesse's my twin."

With a grin, Ceili looked in the same direction Justin did. "Fraternal, obviously."

The two had a strong family resemblance, both had the same kind of lean features. Both had similar dark brown hair, with strong eyebrows of the same color, and the same firm mouth. Jesse, though, had blue eyes while Justin's were more hazel. Given Justin's lean muscular frame beneath his paramedic's uniform, she wondered if Jesse was built the same. It was hard to tell under Jesse's gear.

Life was not fair. Both were too damn handsome.

She looked down at Ranger, the only male in her life for years, who sat on the ground next to her, leaning against her leg. She stroked his head.

"And who is this?" Justin asked, going to one knee in front of the dog.

The simple gesture thoroughly endeared him to her.

Ranger eyed him.

"Shake, Ranger," she said.

Obediently, the dog offered a paw.

With a smile, Justin took it, then stroked a hand over Ranger's head.

Ceili resisted the urge to do the same to the man, wondering what that rich brown hair with its slight wave would feel like.

"Good boy, Ranger," she said, softly.

She looked toward the apartment building, and her lower floor apartment. The windows were broken out, smoke stains visible above them. Her apartment had been just above the laundry and storage area. The first time she'd seen those spaces, she'd thought 'fire hazard' but she couldn't stop people from adding to it.

Her neighbors, those she'd been able to awaken and those evacuated by the firefighters, were gathered in a loose knot, watching as the firefighters tried to put the fire out. Like her, all of them were wondering what they'd be able to recover. She sighed. By the looks of her apartment, not much. Smoke, soot, steam from the water they were pouring onto the fire, and the water itself, would pretty much destroy everything.

Then with relief she saw them bring the Monaghan kids around from the side of the building. Two boys and a girl, looking frightened but unharmed. Then they got closer.

"Ranger!" Missy Monaghan cried, wriggling in the firefighter's arms. He put her down, and she launched herself at the dog. "Ranger! Ranger!"

The dog gave Ceili a beseeching look.

"Go on, silly dog," she said, with a smile.

The little girl threw her arms around the dog's neck, to bury her face against his fur, her brothers only a step behind.

"Do you need me?" Ceili asked Justin.

"A few more questions," he said. "It'll wait."

Justin watched her hurry toward the children, her nightgown just shy of being entirely too short above her shapely legs. She did have an incredible ass, tight and firm.

Deliberately, he took a deep breath. That nightgown was disturbing his own respiration, as were the curves revealed by it.

"Ceili!" the little girl said and burst into tears as Ceili went to one knee, oblivious to the mud.

The little girl's brothers took her place hugging the dog as the little girl hurled herself into Ceili's arms.

"I was so scared," the little girl said. "It was so dark, and I couldn't find my mom and dad."

Lifting her head, Ceili said, "There they are."

The kids ran toward their parents as the mom and dad were helped out of the building.

Firefighters took them toward another ambulance and the paramedics and EMTs there.

Ceili saw the Johnsons, neither looking good, bedraggled, scared, and too pale, being brought out.

She ran to them.

Justin saw her hands moving gracefully as the woman almost visibly sagged at the sight of a familiar face and her moving hands. Her husband looked a bit rockier.

"Ceili," Julie said, relieved. Her hands moved and Ceili nodded.

Looking up at the fireman helping Tony, Ceili saw it was Jesse Armitage. That was a relief. He was already guiding Tony toward Justin's ambulance.

She turned toward Justin. "Tony has asthma," she said. "He's having trouble breathing."

"Tony," she said, waving to get the man's attention then tapping Justin's name on his uniform before signing the rest. "This is Justin. He's a paramedic, he's going to help you."

"Have him sit here, Ceili," Justin said. "Jess, give me a hand with the stretcher, would you?"

With Ceili translating, they got Tony Johnson seated on the stretcher, and then laying on it, his upper body raised enough to make breathing easier, and an oxygen tube helping.

Seeing that, Brian hurried over to help them get the stretcher in the ambulance. "It's just the usual, Justin. A little smoke, nothing major."

With a nod, Justin looked at Ceili regretfully. "You can't ride with them, you're not family. And I still have information for my report to ask you."

"I'll find a way to get to the hospital," she said, looking back at her apartment. How much of the fire had reached it? How much damage had the smoke, water, and steam done? Her car keys were in there, along with all her ID, her credit cards, not to mention her clothes.

He saw the sudden realization of the real impact of her losses in her eyes, and wished he could take her in his arms, give her comfort, but there were the Johnsons.

She looked lost.

"Do you have this, Jess?"

His brother's eyes showed the same concern. Jess nodded at him. "As much as I can."

Reaching out, Justin touched her hand, all the comfort he could offer, before climbing up into the ambulance.

Brian closed the door and hurried to the front of the ambulance to drive.

As much as she appreciated that small gesture from Justin – and she did – the real import of the fire staggered her.

How exactly *was* she going to get to the hospital? Everything was in her now gutted apartment. She doubted that they'd let her back in for a while, it wouldn't be safe, and there still might be hot spots. The firefighters were still going through the building looking for them while others were making sure the fire in the basement was out.

So, she had no clothes but what she was wearing.

For a brief moment she wanted to cry as she realized just how much she had likely lost. All she had was on her, her cell phone, and Ranger.

A hand touched her shoulder.

She looked up to see Jesse standing there. "Which apartment was yours?"

"That one," she said and pointed.

Mentally, Jesse winced. Judging by the location it was the one right above some of the worst of the blaze. The smoke trailing out through the window was thinning.

"Do you mind?" she asked, looking up at him.

It touched Jesse that she asked, her face pale, the golden freckles stark against it, her brilliant blue eyes shining a little too brightly.

He unfastened his turnout jacket – she didn't need to breathe the smoke or soot on it – and shook his head. "Hardly."

Leaning her forehead against his chest, she ran her hands within the coat to clench her hands in his tee shirt beneath it. She took a couple of hitching breaths and he wrapped his arms around her. His tee shirt grew damp, but she never made a sound, simply leaned into him.

The smell of him, a mix of his sweat and soot, filled her, and Ceili breathed him in. It was remarkably soothing. He felt as good as he smelled, she could feel the strength in the broad, curved muscles of his chest, and she needed that desperately. She clung to him, leaning on his strength. The last few years had been like hammer blows for her, this fire was just insult on top of injury.

Even so, she knew she was asking a lot of him. She raised her face to look up at him, into his strong handsome features.

"Thank you," she said, softly. Standing on tip-toe, she kissed his cheek.

Looking down at her, so vulnerable, yet trying hard to hold it together, Jesse was all too aware of her body against his, the firm press of her breasts beneath the thin nightgown against his chest. He was also aware of the other firefighters. Despite that, he still had to fight to resist the urge to take that soft mouth and devour it.

Instead, all he said was, "Anytime," and meant it.

That pretty mouth quirked, and her tear-drenched eyes lightened a little as she heard what he couldn't say.

"Given your signing skills," he said. "I'll check with the Chief to see if we can get you to the hospital to help those deaf folks and get Justin his information so he can finish his report."

He grinned, and Ceili saw the mischief in his eyes. "That'll make it easier on me too. I'll just copy off him."

That made her smile. "Do that a lot, do you?"

With a chuckle, he said, "We used to copy off each other when we were kids."

Then she sighed. "I could wish to be better dressed," she said, plucking at the thin nightgown. "When I went to bed last night, I wasn't expecting to be out in public in this."

Only a little ruefully, he said, "I wish we could help you out there, but the folks from the Red Cross might be able to." Although he couldn't mind too much, given the way it clung to her curves.

"Or someone from the hospital," she said on a sigh. "But what do I do about Ranger?"

For a moment he hesitated. "Let's see what the Chief says. We might be able to keep him at the firehouse until you're done at the hospital."

She gave the dog a side-ways look. "You might regret that offer."

Jesse ruffled Ranger's ears, then scratched behind them. "Oh, I doubt that."

With a wobbly grin she said, "You have no idea."

# Chapter Two

It felt odd not to have Ranger with her, she felt more than a little vulnerable without him and strangely bereft. He was her constant companion. She'd had him since he was six months old, still as much puppy as dog, and she'd helped train him. He'd whined in distress when she'd left him with the fire captain who'd been kind enough to drive her to the hospital. She'd sat in the back with Ranger, to Captain Tate's all too obvious relief. She'd noticed a few of the firefighters trying manfully not to ogle her in the short nightgown, and a few who hadn't even tried. She couldn't blame either, although the explanation for why she wore it would have been even more discomforting.

She could have wished it had been Jesse or Justin who'd driven her, but both had other duties.

"Just keep an eye on him," she told Captain Tate as she got out of the car. She gave him a chagrined look. "He's stressed, and when he's stressed he'll try to eat the firehouse. And I'm not kidding. He tried to eat my couch once."

"It's only for a few hours," Captain Tate said warily.

She rolled her eyes. "You have no idea." She shook her finger at Ranger. "You behave yourself, silly dog."

He just looked at her mournfully.

"Sorry, baby," she said, and hugged him.

"Roll the window up," she said. "Or he'll try to follow me."

She turned toward the ER entrance. As she did, she heard Ranger barking frantically and her heart nearly broke, but she couldn't take him where she was going. Hospitals weren't big on dogs.

Several of the staff were clearly scandalized by her scanty attire, but Ceili couldn't do anything about that.

It took a lot of explaining, until Justin Armitage appeared. He'd clearly been looking for her. She was so grateful to see him. Finally, she might able to help Julie and Tony.

*****

Justin had been wondering where she was, the Johnsons were frantic, and he still had questions to ask to fill out his reports. When Jesse texted to tell him she'd been dropped off at the ER, he'd gone out to the waiting room in search of her.

In a way, he couldn't blame the staff for their hesitation, she had smudges of smoke and ash on her face, including the tip of her nose, her hair was a bit disheveled, and she was still wearing that little and now much-battered nightgown. He couldn't help admiring the way it displayed all her lovely, lush curves and her tight ass above those gorgeous legs.

With an effort he brought his attention back to the matter at hand.

"There you are, Miss Whelan," he said.

At the sound of his voice, she turned to look at him, and smiled warmly to see him but he also saw relief in her blue eyes. God, she was pretty. Her eyes sparkled at the formal address. "The Johnsons need you, and I still have a few questions." He looked at the hospital check in staff. "Miss Whelan is a neighbor of the Johnsons, she was in the fire, too. She knows sign language, though, so she can translate for them. I'll vouch for her, if that will help."

"Thank you," she said, gratefully and fervently as they passed through the ER doors. She grinned wryly. "I think they were going to call the cops on me."

"As it happens, I know one, my brother Caleb. He would
have sprung you loose," he said, wondering what Caleb
would think of that call if he'd had to make it, smiling back.
"So, you're safe. I just have a few quick easy questions."

He could have wished his questions took longer, he liked
looking at her expressive face, but he had the answers for his
report before they reached the door.

A voice over his radio called him back to work.

Judging by her expression and the moment of hesitation,
she was just as reluctant to see him go as he was to leave, but
he was on call and the Johnsons needed her.

"I have to go," he said. "Take care of yourself, Ceili, let
me know if there's anything I can do to help."

Ceili watched him walk away with a sigh, then turned to
Tony Johnson's room.

"We couldn't reach the sign language interpreter," the
nurse explained, as Julie just about burst into tears at the sight
of Ceili peering around the door.

The staff had resorted to writing things on a clipboard,
which took longer for even the simplest statements or
requests. It was clear both Julie and Tony were at their wits
end.

For the next few hours or so she explained complex
medical terms – sometimes having to resort to asking the staff
for a more detailed description – for why they wanted to keep
Tony as they moved him to a room rather than releasing him.
Some of his blood tests had come back with some anomalies
and they were trying to determine what the cause was.

Then, to her astonishment, Justin Armitage appeared as if
from nowhere while the doctor was examining Tony again.
Despite her sign language skills, she wasn't family and all
Tony had on was a hospital robe.

"Justin," she said in surprise, "what are you doing here?"

"This," Justin handed her the bag in his hand. "I had to guess at sizes."

As much as that damned nightgown revealed, it was going to be the death of him, Justin thought. He'd gone on another run – a possible heart attack – and found her the subject of a lot of comment on the part of the hospital staff, so he'd peered down the hall to see her wearing the same much-besmudged, and far too revealing, nightdress. As much as he enjoyed the view, he really didn't want her to have to share it – or all her lovely curves – with everyone.

So as soon as he was off shift, he'd stopped at a store near the hospital.

Ceili glanced inside the bag and her breath caught. She almost burst into tears. It was just a tee shirt and jeans, but there were panties and a bra also. Pretty, lacy panties and a bra in a brilliant blue.

"Ohhhh." She breathed, then looked up at him. "I don't know when I'll be able to pay you back," she said.

It was true. Her credit cards, ID, everything would need to be replaced. Some of it wouldn't happen quickly either, especially without a computer or laptop. It suddenly all threatened to crash over her, as well as all the things she'd need to do to get it all back.

Justin saw the brief shimmer of brightness in her eyes. All things considered, the fire, the loss of almost everything she owned, she'd been showing a remarkable steadiness he could only admire. It was good to see a crack in that armor.

"Don't worry about it," he said. "I think I can manage that much."

Throwing her arms around his neck in gratitude, Ceili gave him a smacking kiss right on the mouth.

It caught Justin off guard, but at the feel of her mouth on his, Justin returned the gesture, with interest. And more. He'd been attracted to her almost from the first moment he'd seen her, not just for all those lovely curves, but her humor, her unselfconsciousness, and her kindness – remembering her going to her knee, oblivious to the mud, for the little girl. That she was just as oblivious to his attraction to her was also clear.

Now though? Attraction flared into something more.

Damn but the girl tasted clean, clear, and sweet. Her mouth on his was soft at first, and then he felt the fire in her as she responded. Everything went away but the feel of her mouth on his, of her body, all those lovely curves pressed against him. On this floor they didn't know him, but even if they had, he wouldn't have cared. Her lips parted on a breath, and he drove his fingers into her hair to pull her mouth harder against his.

It had been impulse for Ceili to kiss him, she was so grateful he'd bought her the clothes. Now she drowned in the feel of his mouth against hers. It seemed like forever since anyone had kissed her, much less with such passion. A passion and desire she shared. And then he had her pressed against the wall, his hips driving against hers and she could feel every inch of him. The long hard length of him. A need and a want she'd suppressed for so long suddenly exploded to life once again.

A voice called from within Tony's hospital room. "Miss Whelan…"

It summoned her back to reality. The doctor. Tony's doctor. Her head was spinning.

"Thank you," she said, and wasn't sure if she was thanking him for the clothes or the kiss. That kiss had rocked her soul. "I have to go."

Ceili looked up into Justin's handsome face. Those entrancing amber eyes and the feel of his body against hers were a forbidden fruit and a sweet torture.

She didn't want to, yet she had to, and not just because of Tony. She couldn't put anyone in the middle of her life, not now. And it wasn't just Justin. She remembered all too well the look in Jesse's eyes, and the sudden sharp sense of desire for him that was just as strong as what she felt for Justin.

The truth was, though, that she couldn't, shouldn't, get involved with either of them. And not just because they were brothers, twins, but because of the mess her life had become.

She'd done the right thing, but no one had imagined the price would be so very, very high, or that it would go on so far beyond what it should have. It should have been over after the trial, but it hadn't been. It still wasn't and there were times she thought it never would be.

"Go do what you need to," he said. "I'll see you later."

Ceili didn't want to tell him no, he wouldn't, but she couldn't. It would take too long to explain, and she sensed something in him, a sense of honor and determination, that wouldn't be denied that explanation.

As much as she wanted to take the comfort he offered, she knew she couldn't.

She watched him go, striding down the hall, and wished she could call him back, even knowing she shouldn't.

As if he felt her eyes on him, he glanced back once. Those eyes… her heart skipped a beat. Then he was gone.

"Coming, Doctor," she said and sighed.

*****

The sign-language interpreter the hospital used finally responded, relieving Ceili of that duty. Not that she really minded. Julie and Tony were good people, but she had yet to find a place to stay herself. She'd called the Red Cross, they were checking their records to find her a place, one willing to take a dog. She wouldn't even consider putting Ranger in a kennel, not that she had the money to do it. They would call her back soon, they promised, and they'd send someone wherever she was with information and help. She just needed to help them fill out some forms. Then they'd give her vouchers for the room and a bank card with enough money on it to carry her for the weekend.

She also to rescue the fire station from the dog. With a grin she thought Ranger was probably keeping the firefighters very busy when they weren't out on a call, if only to keep him from eating half the station.

If Jesse was still on, then he could tell Justin what was happening with her. It was better, safer, that way.

The memory of Justin's kiss was still vivid in her mind. As was her intense attraction to him. She still couldn't believe it.

Even so, in her mind's eye, she could see Jesse in his turn-out gear and wondered what he looked like without the helmet, jacket and protective pants. She remembered his blue eyes, though, and the feel of the muscles of his chest.

One of the nurses going off-shift was kind enough to give her a lift to Jesse's fire station.

She walked in to find Ranger happily sprawled on the couch. He was matched by some of the firefighters, each of which was ensconced in a recliner and pretty zonked out.

"Silly beast," she said.

The dog opened his eyes a crack, decided he didn't want to leave, and closed them again.

Bemused, she looked from dog to people.

"What did you do to my dog?" she asked, softly, amused. "Or better yet, what did he do to you?"

She hadn't intended to be answered, but she was.

From behind her, his deep voice soft, Jesse chuckled. "They had a grand time," he said, shaking his head. "That dog wore them all out. First by stealing the pillows off the couch."

She turned to look at him. A mistake but not a bad one. Her heart fluttered. Like Justin, he was just too gorgeous, but in his own way. Where Justin had hazel eyes that were almost gold, his were blue-gray. She liked seeing them twinkle with mischief. Justin had a lean strength to him, while Jesse had more defined muscle. His tee-shirt and uniform slacks couldn't hide his broad shoulders or the strong curves of his chest, or the ripple of his abs. A part of her wanted to span her hands across that chest, to feel the muscle there again. She took a deep breath and tried to push the thought away.

Even so, she hadn't missed what he said.

"How many did he eat?" she asked with a wince.

With a grin, he opened one of the doors to the back of the station. "Just the one, but one was enough."

It had been. Pillow stuffing was scattered or blowing across the parking area and the grass around it. She could too easily see Ranger happily playing keep away while tossing and shaking his head to send the contents of the pillow flying in every direction.

"Oh, my…"

"We learned pretty fast after that not to leave that dog alone for a second. And to keep an eye on him constantly after Joe left the refrigerator door open just long enough for Ranger to steal a whole package of brats, which he went through in seconds."

Ceili could hear smothered laughter in his deep voice.

Laughter warred with guilt. "I'm so sorry, really I am. I give him cheap hot dogs as treats, but break them into pieces, otherwise he'd swallow them whole and still want more."

"He does and did. He had the plastic off in one bite. Then they discovered he liked chasing balls, wrestling them for it, playing tug," Jesse said as he let the door close. "He wore them out before they wore him out. That dog has energy. How do you keep up with him?"

"Sometimes I don't. I'll take him for runs at the reservoir, play frisbee with him, and take him to an obstacle course." She laughed, eyeing the comfortable dog and shaking her head ruefully. "Now I'll never be able to keep him off the furniture."

Jesse found he missed the little nightgown and the way it had draped over her curves, but the color of the tee shirt brought out the blue in her eyes, made them even brighter in her pretty face with its dusting of freckles. It was also just a little snug across her breasts, dipping in at her waist. The jeans fit just right, though, making the most of her firm ass. One thing for certain, that dog kept her nicely toned.

"Did the Red Cross come through?" he asked, with a nod at her clothing.

She blushed a little, which made her freckles almost disappear, except for the dusting of gold across her nose. Abashed, her mouth quirked and she gestured at the tee shirt and jeans. "No, your brother took pity on me and bought these for me, bless his heart. It was getting embarrassing to be running around half-naked and I smelled of smoke. I still do, I think."

She sniffed at her arm, and ran her fingers through her hair, wrinkling her nose.

That mobile, expressive mouth of hers was distracting. All he had to do was watch that mouth to know her mood. What astonished him was that she was clueless about how pretty she was, how very attracted he was to her.

"It happens, we deal with it all the time. Need a shower? We have a women's locker room. I'll stand guard, if you'd like. Come with me."

For a shower Ceili would have followed him anywhere. At just the thought of getting clean, she sighed in relief. "Oh, that would be wonderful. I'm pretty sure my hair smells, too. Bless you." As they came to a stop she went up on tip-toe, intending to kiss him on the cheek, but he turned his head at exactly the wrong – or the right – moment to look down at her. Her kiss hit him squarely on the mouth.

For only a heartbeat, Jesse hesitated, then he yanked the door open – knowing none of the women firefighters were on this shift – and backed her inside, his hands cupped around that tight ass. He devoured her mouth, crushing it beneath his.

He'd wanted to do this since the first moment he'd gotten a really good look at her, the engine lights and the rising sun sparking red highlights in that tumbled, pretty mop of sunset hair, the dusting of freckles over her finely featured face. She had the slightest bump in her nose, as if it had been broken at some time, but that and the scar in her eyebrow were oddly endearing.

As was her surprise when his mouth took hers.

Now, tasting her, feeling her lips respond to his, he traced the seam between them with his tongue, and she opened to him with a sigh.

That soft sound was all he needed, he lifted her to drive his hips against hers. She wrapped her legs around his and he hefted her higher, to drive his hardening cock against her.

It might be a mistake, Ceili knew, but she couldn't stop herself from making it any more than she could with his brother. And, oh, how she needed it. Needed to touch, to hold and be held.

Jesse was fierce where Justin was intent, though both were just as intense, just as passionate in their own way.

She could feel his hardening length pressed against her mound, she rode it and him, her hips shifting. Need and desire were an aching tension inside her, a heat that grew as he took possession of her mouth. One hand cupped her ass to keep her from sliding down the wall, the other skimmed down her throat, traced her collarbone, and found her breast.

Jesse heard her gasp even as his hand closed over the fullness of her, the tip of her breast hardening beneath his palm.

He groaned as she arched into his hand, pressing her breast, so firm, so full, against it.

This wasn't the time or the place, though. If he was away too long, someone would notice. He didn't want an audience. It also broke about a dozen rules.

Reluctantly, he lifted his mouth from hers and took a breath. "God, I want you, but not here, not this way."

That stunned her. Ceili looked up at him to see the desire in his eyes. For her? Her breath caught. He couldn't have said what she thought he said.

It was also a badly needed dash of cold water. She couldn't, shouldn't.

"I want you, too," she said, softly, her voice still a little husky with desire and need. She did, a part of her wanted him badly, just as badly as she wanted his brother. And she couldn't. "But you're probably right."

Had she really kissed both brothers? She had and she wanted them, both of them, each of them. Given the choice she couldn't have picked one over the other. However wrong, it was the truth. Not that it mattered, she couldn't have either, she had other problems... It simply wasn't an option, even if he had meant it.

"I'll let you take your shower," he said. "I'll be right outside."

She nodded, caught between longing and relief, trying to clear her head.

And what about his brother, his twin? So different, despite being born within what was probably minutes of each other. She was drawn to him as well. It wasn't fair to either. But she couldn't choose and didn't want to. She did want to get to know them better. Which was something she couldn't do. The weight of her need, her loneliness, was crushing.

Taking a breath, she turned toward the showers.

They were institutional, but they were clean, and that was enough. She had bathed in far worse.

She hoped whoever had left their shampoo and soap wouldn't mind her using them. They did smell good, and a lot better than the smoky smell that seemed to permeate her skin and hair. It took only a moment to strip out of her clothes and step into the steaming water. It also felt wonderful to get clean.

It didn't seem like someplace she should linger, though. She wasn't certain of the protocol of letting a civilian use the facilities. Or whether Jesse would get in trouble for letting her.

Her cell phone, the only thing she'd salvaged from the fire, rang as she dried her hair, finger-combing it into place around her face, scrunching the rest.

She picked up the phone. "Ceili," she said.

"Miss Whelan? This is Marcie with the Red Cross. We've found a temporary place for you and your dog, at least until you can find something better. Where are you right now?"

A part of her heart sank, even as relief went through her. She wanted a bit more time with Jesse, but it was probably better this way. And she still needed somewhere to sleep whatever happened.

She gave the name and address of the firehouse. "It's Station Eleven of the Fire Department."

"We're sending someone to you with the information, a voucher for the hotel and a bank card. There's a thrift shop near the motel we work with that will supply you with some clothes."

"That's wonderful," she said, trying to infuse more gratitude into her tone, although her heart ached at what she wished could have been. It couldn't be, no matter how much she wanted it to be otherwise. She sighed.

"Thank you so much," she said, and tried to sound properly enthusiastic. "I'll be waiting."

She hung up, dressing as quickly as she could, but she was also aware that a part of her was dragging it out so she wouldn't have to say goodbye to Jesse.

Walking out of the shower, she found him leaning against the wall and couldn't help smiling. It wasn't just his looks, either, it was the warmth in his eyes and the kindness he'd shown her after the fire. He hadn't had to do that and probably shouldn't have. The sight of his long strong body didn't hurt. The muscles in his chest and shoulders showed clearly through his tee shirt, as it did in his bared arms.

"That was quick," he said, surprised.

She tousled her hair. "The blessing of the short cut, it dries quickly. I grew it longer once upon a time."

Taking a handful of it, watching the heat in her eyes kindle, Jesse said, "It's still a little damp."

He pulled her closer.

Ceili took a breath, wishing it could be different, but it wasn't. Dear God, she wanted him. She lifted her fingers to his mouth to stop him, fighting her own desire.

"The Red Cross called while I was in the shower. They have a temporary place for me and Ranger, I just have to fill out some forms for them."

Jesse could see regret and sorrow shadow her bright eyes. He wished… but he was still on duty for a few more hours. He was on a twenty-four-hour shift.

"Call me when you know where?" he asked. "Just leave a message for me here at the station. I'll call back."

She wanted to tell him the truth, she wanted to lean into his strength, she wanted to be honest with him… but she couldn't. It wasn't safe or fair.

Instead, she did what she wanted to do, what she knew he wanted from her, and dragged his head and mouth down to hers, kissing him with all her heart and soul. Then she cupped his face, looking at him, holding the image of him in her mind before stepping back.

"I hate to go, but I have to," she said, and that was nothing more than the truth.

She whirled away from him, before she did anything more she might regret. It wasn't fair to him to lead him on or to lie to him.

"Ranger, come!"

The dog bounded into the hallway, his eyes bright, locked on her.

Glancing back over her shoulder at Jesse, her heart aching, she stepped out of the station.

A car with the symbol of the Red Cross on it was waiting. A tall bald man with a broad, kind, round face stepped out of it.

"Ceili Whelan?" he asked.

"That would be me," she said.

"I'm Christopher," he said, "but you can call me Chris."

"Hi, Chris," she said, and gave him a look. "And it's Ceili. Shorten it to Cei and I'll have to hurt you."

Chuckling he said, "All right then. This place we found for you, it's sort of a no-tell motel, but it's only temporary until you or we find someplace better. They were willing to take the dog and not many places will. I have a dog myself, so I brought some food for him with me. Not much, just enough to get him through tonight. Just don't tell anyone." He winked at her.

"Thank you," she said gratefully. "As for the motel? Beggars can't be choosers."

"Let's get this information filled out," he said. "Then I can give you the cards and vouchers. I'm afraid I can't transport you, it's against the rules. You'll have to arrange that yourself."

"Give me a second first, and I'll call a ride service."

By the time the ride service arrived, they had the forms filled in and she had the location of the motel and the thrift shop.

"Here's a bank debit card and the motel voucher. Use the card sparingly, there's not much on it, so keep that in mind."

"Thanks, Chris, I really appreciate it."

She opened the back door of the ride service car and Ranger scrambled into the seat, stretching out to make himself comfortable.

She ruffled his ears. "Don't mess with that bag, you hear me?"

Now that she had pointed it out to him, his ears perked up.

Rolling her eyes at him, she slid in beside the driver.

Both of them heard the bag tear and Ranger happily munching. Ceili banged her head lightly against the window.

"I think he found it," the driver said, amused.

She looked back at Ranger. He just looked at her, his eyes bright with mischief. "Ya think?" she said, laughing lightly. "Silly beast. Heaven give me strength."

The motel was about what Chris had said, a no-tell motel, rundown and faded. She asked for and got a second-floor end room far away from the neighbors.

It was a place to sleep. She'd manage. After all, what choice did she have? She'd slept in worse.

For the first time in what seemed forever, Ceili wished she could have talked to Chris for a little longer, or the ride service driver. She was suddenly and acutely aware of how alone she was. She tried not to think of Jesse and Justin, their kindness, although just the thought of them was enough to make her heart wrench. She sighed.

Tucking the bag under one arm, she opened the door to the motel room.

As shabby as the rest, it wasn't impressive. A cheap print on the wall, privacy curtains on the windows, and a carpet that had seen much better days. She took one look at the bed and resolved never to sleep on the thing. She went in hunt of spare clean linens. A spare blanket and pillow were on a shelf in the closet. She spread the blanket over the couch and put the bag with the dog food in its place. Ranger looked up at her with interest, eyeing the bag. She closed the door firmly.

Ceili gave him a fond but warning look, ruffling his ears.

Her phone lasted a while on battery, but she no longer had a charger, so she didn't dare use it much. Something else she'd have to replace somehow. The reality of her situation threatened to overwhelm her. Sensing it, Ranger hopped up beside her to lay his head in her lap for consolation. Part of her wished for another kind of companionship, but she resolutely left the phone silent.

She needed a distraction, so she flicked on the TV.

To her surprise, they were showing the aftermath of the fire. Had it only been that morning?

She found herself searching the images for a sight of familiar forms and faces. It wasn't her neighbors she looked for. In his turnout gear, Jesse was just another of the firefighters. She was blind to the sight of herself, but the camera caught a glimpse of Justin and her heart ached. She wished he was here, that she could curl up in his arms.

She fought the urge to call either of them, however much she wanted to.

For the first time in a long time, she was aware of how lonely she was. Her heart ached. She hugged Ranger and buried her face in his fur.

# Chapter Three

Somehow, Jesse knew Ceili wouldn't call. Something in her eyes, regret and sorrow, told him she wouldn't but he kept hoping she'd change her mind. Justin was just as distracted as he was. Not a surprise, after a run, he'd gone to check to see if she was still at the hospital, and found she was. He'd told Jesse before he'd gone off shift that he was going to get the girl some decent clothes.

"You two are pretty quiet tonight," Caleb said, eyeing his younger brothers.

Neither was really watching the TV, but nothing much was on anyway.

They shared the four-bedroom condo. Splitting the bills made it cheaper for all of them and gave them a good place to crash. Each had their own space and the extra bedroom was now their exercise room. Jesse had commandeered the basement.

Jesse took a breath. "We got called out to a fire this morning. An apartment building."

Nodding, Caleb said, "I saw it on TV. They said the fire alarms didn't work, but one of the residents went back in, roused everyone and got them out. A girl… woman. That was either incredibly stupid, or incredibly brave."

"Ceili Whelan. Brave," Jesse said, distractedly. "She's got courage, that's for sure. And enough presence of mind to tell us who hadn't made it out yet, making our job a lot easier. Two of them were deaf."

"So, she translated what we needed into sign language for them," Justin said.

Caleb heard the subtext. He was getting the picture. Both were clearly attracted, so this girl was undoubtedly attractive, but there was something more to it than just that. This woman had clearly impressed both his brothers. "What's she like? Besides being either brave or stupid."

"Not stupid," Justin said, "or just a little. She did call it in first. Going back inside was more dangerous than she probably knew, but it was still a hell of a gutsy thing to do. Even so, the smoke would have blinded her, she could easily have died. It was surprising she didn't. On top of that she lost everything to the fire."

Shaking his head, with a half laugh, Jesse added, "Everything except that damn dog. It looks like a small German Shepherd, has enough energy to wear out a crew of firefighters and eat a pillow left on the fire station couch. Took off with it and shredded the thing in seconds. Plus wolfing down Jeff's bratwurst. He's going to be pissed to find them gone. More so that a dog got them."

"Yet she just kept going, like the Energizer bunny," Justin said. "She stayed at the hospital, translating, until she was sure her neighbors didn't need her anymore. And she's pretty, Caleb, with hair that's sort of golden red, and blue eyes that just wreck you. And, although she didn't intend it the way it turned out, she kisses like no one's business."

That her looks were an afterthought, Caleb thought, said a lot about how impressed Justin was by the woman.

"Yeah, she does that," Jesse agreed. It neither surprised nor bothered him that Justin had kissed her, too. They might be fraternal twins, but they had similar tastes in women. It was no surprise that Justin had been as attracted to her as he was. They had shared a lot over the years, just not a woman. Not that way. Not many would have gone for it. That she was clearly attracted to them both, though, had his mind going in interesting directions.

"Both of you?" Caleb said. "Playing one against the other?" It wouldn't have been the first time a woman had done that to his brothers, knowing they were twins, even if they were fraternal. People tended to romanticize the twin thing. He'd seen his brothers get messed up by a few women over the years, the woman going from one to the other, comparing one against the other. A spark of anger went through him at the thought.

With one arm curled behind his head, Justin stretched out on the couch, his feet hanging over the end and shook his head. "It wasn't like that, Caleb. That's happened often enough now that Jess and I know the signs. But all she had to wear was this little nightgown. It barely covered her ass."

"And what an ass," Jesse said, his admiration of it evident. "Of course, she gets a lot of exercise from that dog. Ranger." He smiled. "That dog is too smart by half."

"By the end of the night that little nightgown was covered in soot, ash, and mud," Justin said. The memory of the way it had clung to her curves, the bottom of it swishing above her shapely legs made his cock stiffen again. "Not that it bothered her much, she didn't have much choice, and knew it. So I bought her some decent clothes, she needed something else to wear. Just jeans and a tee shirt." He didn't mention the lacy bra or panties he'd bought, too, but wondering how they fit wasn't helping him any. His cock was nearly rigid at the thought. "Nothing much, but she was so grateful she kissed me. It's as if she wasn't used to someone being nice to her. I don't think she intended it to be more than that, just a quick kiss, that was all me. It caught me off guard, but I already wanted her. She impressed the hell out of me both during and after the fire, and then there's that hair, her eyes, and that body. The woman has some great curves."

Jesse nodded. "I let her use the women's showers at the station. She started to kiss me on the cheek, but like Justin I wanted more. It surprised her, but then she just went with it. I'm not sure now which of us wanted that kiss most, her or me." He was quiet for a moment. The feel of her body, her responsiveness. That hunger. "The Red Cross found her a temporary place to stay. I asked her to call me, tell me where. I got the impression she wanted to… But she hasn't."

"Then she's told you where she stands," Caleb said.

Jesse traded a look with his twin. Neither he nor Justin believed that was the whole story.

"I don't think so," he said, "There's something else going on there."

"Yeah," Justin said, "I got that, too."

But Caleb did sort of have it right. Short of hunting her down, there was nothing they could do unless she asked for help. And it was becoming clear she wasn't going to do that.

*****

Morning dawned bright, so Ceili walked Ranger down the street to one of the chain coffee shops. She got a coffee and two breakfast sandwiches, giving Ranger the other. They'd passed the phone store for her service. After hearing her story, they took pity on her, allowed her to bring Ranger inside and loaned her a charger. Plugged in to the shop, she reported her charge cards as missing in the fire, requested replacements be delivered to the bank, then did the same for her driver's license for pickup at the DMV.

The first hang-up call came later that day while she was walking Ranger. Ceili went still, looking around her quickly. Nothing, yet, to raise any alarms. She looked at the display. Unknown number. She took a deep breath.

It could be innocent. A robo-caller. Political or a business. She looked at the display, let it ring but didn't answer.

Another came in Sunday night. Ringing and ringing. She didn't answer, but it alarmed her. All the caller ID said was 'reserved number'.

Fear shot through her. Maybe it was nothing. Maybe it wasn't. She had no time for fear.

Running wasn't an option. Out in the open, with only Ranger? Not knowing if someone was out there? Or where they were.

She wasted no time, pushing the heavy dresser over by the closet near the door. In the shadows away from the windows. Dragging the mattress off the bed, she laid it against the dresser, creating a barrier of sorts. One of the chairs she propped beneath the doorknob. She could do nothing about the windows. Taking the clean blanket from the couch, she spread it out onto the floor behind her makeshift wall.

Quickly, she turned the lights out.

"Ranger," she said, and he came to her, eyes alert, head up.

Maybe it was nothing. Maybe she was just being paranoid about a wrong number. But if she wasn't? If they'd found her again? Fear ran through her like ice water in her veins.

The first time they'd thought it would be easy to take her, and it nearly was. Absently, she traced the little bump that was the only sign of the break in her nose. But someone had seen and call the police. When they arrived, her attackers had run. That time, it had been street thugs, addicts willing to do anything for fix. Except get arrested.

Someone else tried to run her off the road. The third time had been the break-in at her apartment.

According the local cops, it was just a run of bad luck. She shouldn't have been walking back to her car at night alone. They hadn't known about the near car 'accident'. Or what she'd heard the men say during the break in. It wasn't going to stop. And it hadn't. It had only been luck that no one else had been badly hurt. Yet.

Luck didn't last forever.

Why wouldn't they just leave her alone? She was no threat to them, or to anyone. What had been done was done. It didn't make any sense, except their boss wanted her to die. Eventually. He needed an example made. Just the thought sent something another rush of fear through her.

Beside her, Ranger bristled, hearing something she couldn't.

At that, she was already dialing 911.

"911 operator, what is your emergency?"

The gunfire startled not only her but the 911 operator, the sheer ferocity of it, as windows shattered and someone tried to shoot out the lock, then threw himself against the door. For the moment, the chair held. It wouldn't for long. And there were the windows, hidden now by the privacy curtain that showed shimmers of light through holes that hadn't been there while glass sparkled on the floor beneath them in the light from the streetlight outside.

"Shots fired, shots fired," the 911 voice said. "Where are you. Name and location?"

"The Liberty Motel," Ceili said. "My name is Ceili Whelan. I'm at the Liberty Motel. End unit, second floor."

More shots, more glass shattering as Ceili cried out, her fingers locked tight around Ranger's collar.

"Automatic weapon fire. Stay where you are, Ceili," the 911 operator said. "Officers are responding."

The man outside the door threw himself against it again, as the chair wobbled.

Another tried to look in past the privacy curtains and shattered glass. She saw the movement, saw when he blocked the light. He looked for surprises, for her, but she and Ranger were in the shadows by the closet, concealed behind her makeshift barrier. He bashed out some of the remaining glass with what looked like the barrel of his gun by the pale light of the streetlights. Soon he'd be inside.

"Hurry," she whispered into the phone. "Please hurry."

Luck didn't last forever, she thought again. Had her luck finally run out? She was terrified it had.

She held Ranger behind the barrier, waiting until the last, best minute.

Blue and red lights flashed. Police. She closed her eyes.

A moment of silence. Then she heard a chatter of gunfire.

*****

Marty, Paul's senior partner, brought their cruiser to a stop at the scene of the report of gunfire, even as another pulled up beside them. Although Paul was new on the force after a couple tours in Afghanistan and Iraq and just out of training, he already knew reports of gunfire in this part of town weren't that unusual. A drug deal gone bad, a domestic, or a quarrel over almost anything, and guns came out.

All was quiet, though, and there was no immediate sign of anyone.

Even so, both he and Marty exited their cruiser with their hands on the butts of their weapons and approached the hotel warily, with Marty just slightly ahead of him.

A few cars were parked in the spaces and a semi was stretched lengthwise along the back of the lot, engine rumbling.

Both Marty and he were alert for trouble.

From behind one of the parked cars a man in full military armor suddenly stood up an MP 5 automatic rifle in hand and opened fire.

"What the fuck?" Marty was hit square in the chest, shoulder and arm even as Paul dove for cover.

"Shots fired, shots fired, officer down," he shouted into his radio, then fired a few rounds at the shooter while he scrambled to drag Marty behind cover.

The man retreated to the cover of the building, firing at them, as two others stepped out of cover on the second floor to renew their assault on the second-floor room.

From the armor to the maneuvers, everything about it screamed military.

"Be alert," he said into the radio. "The assailants have military experience."

# **Chapter Four**

Caleb had just arrived at headquarters and was just about to change into his uniform when the SWAT call came in. Instead he ran for the SWAT ARV instead as Jax, Bear, and the rest of his team came running. He threw open the door, grateful he was stationed at one of the few locations that had an ARV and swung inside with the others. Bill hit lights and siren as he got them out on the road.

"What have we got?" Caleb said into his radio.

"Shots fired at the Liberty Street motel. A potential hostage situation. While the vic was talking the 911 operator heard automatic weapons fire. Squads responded, an officer is down on scene. One of the officers said the assailants seem to have military experience."

These days, with so many military-style weapons out there, semi-automatic and automatic weapons fire wasn't that uncommon. He could be grateful that at least it wasn't a school, bar, mall, or office building. All of them had seen the videos of the aftermath of some of those, learned from it and done the training but those videos had been horrific. Some had been a bloodbath.

Caleb knew the Liberty Motel, though. It wasn't the best of places, but the number of tenants there could vary.

"Got it," he said and turned to his team. "One vic inside, automatic weapons fire. How many perps and what they want, we don't know. It's the Liberty Motel, some of you may know it, an old rundown motel on 11$^{th}$ – all rooms open to the front, so it may be straightforward. One of the officers responding is down, another reported that whoever these people are, they have military training or seem to."

Everyone nodded, going more alert.

They killed the lights and siren before they reached the staging area, a nearby coffee shop, now closed so whoever was shooting wouldn't be warned of their arrival.

All the activity seemed to be taking place on the second level, end unit. Someone was trying to kick the door open, another was just going in the window. Below, from the cover of the corner in front of the stairs, someone sprayed the parking lot to keep the officers there from responding. The cruisers lights were shattered.

The parking lot was almost completely open save for a semi.

"Jax, Morgan?"

They nodded.

As the sniper for the team, and the officer in charge Caleb took point, the rest of the team covering as they exited the vehicle, Jax and Morgan flanking them as they raced for cover behind the semi.

The reporting officer hadn't been wrong, everything about these men shouted military, from the man on the lowest floor guarding the stairs and providing cover for those above to the actions of those on the second.

As if sensing their presence, the man on the ground popped his head around the wall and opened fire, spraying bullets across the parking lot. Everyone took cover as the man strafed their positions with automatic weapons fire as he backed toward the stairs to the upper level.

He was Caleb's target.

With full armor there were only a few weak spots, but one primary one.

He lined up his shot, set himself, and fired. Once, twice.

The assailant's head snapped back, and he went down.

From the upper level they heard a cry and gunfire, as one of the men cleared then breached the window.

Now they had cover, another possible target or a potential hostage.

The other kicked in the door.

Caleb swore.

Above them it sounded as if all hell broke loose.


Ceili held until the last minute, crouched behind her barrier, just as Tom – the man who'd trained both her and Ranger – had instructed. One of the men stretched a leg through the window, then shouldered his way into the room. The chair beneath the door wobbled, toppled.

She unleashed the dog, letting go of his collar.

The men hadn't expected a fight or the darkened room, although they had flashlights clipped to their body armor. They were clearly expecting to find her cowering on or under the bed, in a corner or in the bathroom as that's where their flashlights pointed.

Instead, she and Ranger were concealed behind her makeshift barrier by the closet, the mattress and the wood of the dresser scant protection from bullets.

"Get him, Ranger," she whispered, and the dog launched himself across the room at the man who'd come through the windows.

Snarling and growling, the dog leaped to latch onto the man's arm. The man shouted in surprise and then fury, involuntarily pulling the trigger, sending a burst of bullets into where the mattress had been and the wall behind the bed.

Even as he did, another kick to the door sent the door flying open with a crash.

Ranger's motion, his nearly silent sprint and leap at the gun hand of his partner drew the attention of the man who'd broken through the door. His feet tangled with the chair even as he tried to bring his gun around to shoot the dog. The man kicked the chair away even as Ceili ran for him and the door, her eyes only on the barrel of the rifle in his hand. She hit that hand with everything she had, driving it up and away so she could duck beneath it. The gun went off, spraying bullets through the ceiling. Plaster rained down.

The only advantage she had was surprise, and he was between her and escape. That, escape, was her only objective.

The sheer unexpectedness of Ranger, and then her charging at him out of the shadows from a direction he hadn't anticipated caught him off guard, but she knew it was only for a second.

"Ranger, out!" she shouted, even as she ducked and spun away to dart toward the door and through it.

The dog released the other man's arm and shot out in front of her.

She made it outside, collided with the rail, and started to turn to run after Ranger.

A hand tangled in her tee shirt, but she wrapped her arms and a leg around the railing and hung on.

Ranger turned, snarling, to attack even as the man hammered at her with the gun. Pain exploded through her head. The force was blunted, though, by Ranger's attack.

*****

Below, Caleb looked up to see a woman, her reddish hair gleaming in the streetlights, clinging desperately to the railing. A dog savaged the man who was trying to tear her free.

She was in front, between him and the assailant, blocking his shot.

Another man came out, aimed for the dog.

Caleb fired. The man's body armor took some of the force, but it still drove him back a step and threw off his aim.

Looking down, that one saw Caleb's team advancing and snatched at his partner's arm.

The man released the woman, his weapon turning toward her head, but she was already sliding between the rails.

"Ranger," she shouted, scrabbling for purchase on the floor of the walkway. Her fingers gave way and she fell into the scant bushes below. Caleb mentally winced as she hit, as he and others on the team sighted on the men. Her assailant sprayed gunfire where she'd been. They punched into the metal or ricocheted up into the night.

His partner, though, dropped a smoke grenade, another tumbled across the walkway, spewing smoke.

The dog released the man he'd been savaging and sprinted for the stairs.

Under fire, the assailants were more concerned with him and his team than the dog or even the woman now, firing steadily and with military precision as they hurriedly retreated under cover of the smoke.

Returning fire as the assailants fled, Caleb keyed his mic as he and the rest of his team closed in to apprehend the attackers. A van shot across the parking lot, doors open. The men dove inside it even as the driver hit the gas, gunning it for the end of the building.

Caleb swore softly. They'd been prepared for all eventualities. It was startling. These people clearly had military training and had prepared for this, for them. They just hadn't been prepared for the woman and her dog, the dog, at least, also having been military trained.

None of this made sense. Why send a military style unit after a single woman?

"Let's clear that room," he said to his team. With Jax and Bear behind him, they went up the stairs, advanced on the room. Both the other men went low, then faced into the room.

The rest of the team stood at Caleb's back, some covering him, others covering their retreat.

He pushed the door open carefully and warily, but the room was empty. By some miracle one of the lights was still intact. He took in the dresser and the mattress propped against it. The victim had built her own little fort. Scant protection, more concealment. She'd been prepared.

Shaking his head, Caleb said, "What the hell is going on?"

No one had an answer.

"Do a sweep," he said to the rest of the team. "We need make sure there are no more surprises."

He returned to the front of the motel, Bear with him

The dog was crouched over the girl protectively, hackles up, body tense, ears flat.

"Clear," Jax said over the radio.

With a nod, Caleb said into his own mike, "Send the medics, we need paramedics on site. Officer down. Victim is down."

The medic units, waiting at the staging area, hit lights and sirens to get across the highway. He sent one to the downed officer, gestured the other to him.

Caleb wasn't surprised to see his brother appear, they'd left at the same time for their separate stations, and this was the edge of his territory.

"Hey, Caleb," Justin said.

What did surprise Caleb was his brother's next word as he took in the situation.

"Ranger?" Justin asked, puzzled, looking at the dog.

The animal instantly relaxed at the sound of a familiar voice to it, whining, looking up at Justin trustingly.

So, it was Ranger. Justin was stunned. If this was Ranger, then where was Ceili? Ranger lay down beside his mistress, his head on her back.

Justin took one look at Ceili lying sprawled in the mulch and scanty bushes and his heart went cold even as he signaled to his partner. Mike ran to get the backboard and a cervical collar.

"Ceili?" he said, softly, crouching beside her. "Don't move."

At the sound of her name and Justin's familiar, lovely voice, Ceili opened her eyes and tried to turn her head.

"Justin?" She'd been trying to gather her wits about her. The fall had knocked the wind out of her. Between the fall, and the pain at the back of her head, as well as the throbbing of her ankle she struggled to find sense.

His face, those amber eyes, and that firm mouth were unmistakable. She couldn't believe it, but it was him. Maybe it was her imagination. Nothing felt real.

Fear shot through her, those men…

Pain throbbed at the back of her head. Her hand rose to touch it.

Justin caught it. "Stay still, sweetheart," he said softly. "Don't move until I have the chance to check you over."

"He hit me," she whispered. "Hurts."

Blood matted her hair at the back of her head., but scalp wounds bled a lot. At the sight, though, Justin's mouth tightened, and he almost literally saw red at the thought that someone had hit her. Despite that, first things first, she was still his patient and he had to assess her injuries.

"I can see it, Ceili. Just hold still, I have to check to see if there's anything else."

He ran his hands down her neck, her back, then along her shapely legs. She didn't wince or flinch.

He glanced at Caleb in question.

Caleb had been following the exchange between his brother and the victim at the same time he listened over his headset to his team reporting in.

What he hadn't missed was her name, or the endearment. This, then, was the girl, the woman, from the fire. The one who'd caught the attention of both his brothers.

No matter how he looked at it, none of this made any sense.

"I don't know what the hell is going on either, Justin," Caleb said. "We got a call about automatic weapons fire, responded to find two men trying to break into her room, and a third covering them. Everything about them screamed military or ex-military."

"Ex," the girl whispered. "Mercenaries. Drugs. Long story."

Ceili's eyes burned. She was so tired. A tear slid down her cheek. She tried hard not to give way to those tears. She was going to have to run again. She didn't want to run anymore. Tears threatened once again. She pushed them back. Her breath hitched.

"Hush," Justin said, his fingers on her wrist to take her pulse as he watched her breathing.

Understanding what he was doing, what he needed, Ceili wiggled her fingers and toes. Pain shot through her ankle.

"All the parts are working, I think," she said. "I can feel everything. My right ankle hurts."

"Maybe, but we can't take any chances," he said, carefully immobilizing her neck, before he and Mike strapped her into the backboard. "Ready? We're going to roll you over."

"Okay."

For the first time, Caleb got a good look at her as they lifted her and the backboard onto the stretcher. Justin brushed away old mulch and dirt from her face and hair, his small flashlight flicking in front of her eyes to check her pupillary response. His brothers hadn't been wrong about her hair, even in the old dirty streetlights the color was vivid. Her finely featured face was pale but as pretty as his brothers had said, and those blue eyes – tears trembling on the lashes – would tear the heart out of you.

"Wait, Justin," she said. "What about Ranger? I can't leave him."

The dog nuzzled her fingers and whined.

"I'll bring him," Caleb said. "I've got questions."

And she clearly needed to have a protection detail on her.

Those vulnerable eyes went to him. She took a breath, trying to hold it together. He had to admire her courage, thinking of the fragile fort she'd built in her room, her desperate attempt at escape. Even so, she just seemed so normal, there was no hardness to her, no calculation. Compared to what he saw most days she was almost shockingly open.

"I'll try to answer them," she said. "Just please, take care of Ranger? No kennels."

"Ceili," Justin said, to reassure her, as he put a pulse ox sensor on her finger, "Remember when I said I knew a cop? This is him, my older brother Caleb. Caleb, Ceili Whelan."

Looking at Caleb, Ceili could see it. He had a darker version of Justin's amber eyes, the same thick wavy brown hair – although his was a bit lighter – but that mouth. Dear heavens. Her heart stuttered. It was slightly fuller in the upper lip, but firm. He was a sharper, more intense version of his brothers. Except for that mouth.

"Oh my God," she said, blinking. "There's three of you?" It hadn't really registered when Justin had said it the first time, and she hadn't had the reality standing in front of her. She eyed Caleb, tried to shake her head. "I don't know if I can handle three of you."

It would have been more amusing if it hadn't been for the dog.

That dog stood between Caleb, Bear, and pretty, battered Ceili in what was clearly a protective stance. Having seen that dog go after the man who hit her, Caleb wasn't ready to try the dog's temper himself. He eyed the animal warily.

Seeing it, she smiled, a small twist of her mouth. "Sorry, Caleb, it's his training. Stand down, Ranger. Caleb, can you go down to eye level with him? He needs to know you're a friend."

Cautiously, careful not to make too fast a move, Caleb went down on one knee.

"Ranger, shake. That's his safe word, the way to tell him you're a friend."

The dog tilted his head, eyeing Caleb a moment before he obediently offered a paw.

He needed approval from a dog. He almost laughed. But he'd worked with police and military dogs before. It was amusing in a way, it had a purpose, so Caleb took the offer. Unlike most of those other dogs, this one licked his chin. The simple gesture lightened Caleb's mood.

"It seems I've been approved." He smiled and scratched behind the dog's ears. Ranger leaned into his hand.

"I think he likes you," she said, smiling. "Anyone my dog likes, I like. He didn't even blink at Justin, but then he and Jesse don't go armed. Give him simple commands like come, go, etc. Want him to trust someone else? Introduce them. Just don't give him attack words, and don't let him around anything he can chew on, tear apart, or otherwise eat, because he will."

Caleb laughed. "So, Jesse told me."

Embarrassed, she covered her face with her hand. "Oh, no! The damned silly beast is going to be infamous. Caleb, consider yourself warned."

He was, but was it the dog, he had to be careful of, or the woman?

It said a lot about her that, even with a banged head and that fall, she could still find humor in the situation. He was beginning to see what his brothers saw in her, that quirky resilience mixed with vulnerability. It was an intriguing combination. One he was susceptible to himself.

She looked at him. "Promise me. Promise me you'll take care of him? Just until I can get him?"

"He'll be fine," Caleb said, as the dog leaned against his leg. Absently, Caleb stroked the dog's head.

"Let's get you to the hospital to get you checked out," Justin said, with a nod to Mike.

He and Mike rolled her toward the ambulance, lifted and slid her inside.

"He saved me, you know," Ceili said to Justin, her eyes on the dog. She hated leaving him. "Ranger did."

She closed her eyes, let her head fall back as reality took hold again, remembering Ranger leaping for the man who'd come in the window. How close he'd come to being shot. It was going to be hard to be apart from him, especially now when she both felt and was vulnerable.

Looking across at the other unit, she saw the people inside it working over someone with steady determined precision.

"Oh, no," she whispered.

Caleb and Justin both saw her struggle, a tear trickling down her face. He took her hand.

Her chin quivered. "Will he be all right? Please tell me he'll be all right."

"They're doing their best, Ceili," Justin said.

"No one else was supposed to get hurt. It's me they're after."

"It's over," he said.

Her eyes opened, her lashes damp. "No. It's never going to end. I'm so scared, Justin. They just keep coming. Why can't they leave me alone? I'm no threat to anyone, not anymore. I want to fight back, but I can't. It's like fighting a ghost, one who haunts me. And I have to run. Every time I do, they find me again. I don't want to run anymore."

Justin brushed the hair back from her face.

Leaning against the door, Caleb ran a hand over her foot, now bare. "I don't know what to tell you, Ceili, and now isn't the time to talk about it. Just know that for now," he said, "you're safe. Whoever they are will have to go through me and my team to get to you. Not to mention Justin, and from what I hear, Jesse as well. And I'm pretty sure Ranger will have something to say about it, too."

Taking a breath, she laughed lightly. A little shakily, but she laughed. "Or he'll eat my pillow."

Her attempt at humor surprised him. The woman had guts.

Chuckling, he said, "Or that."

"Get the doors, Caleb?" Justin said.

With a nod, Caleb shut them, banged on it to let Mike know it was safe to pull out.

"Let me check that ankle," Justin said.

She had slender, almost coltish ankles, small enough he could have wrapped his fingers around one, so it was easy to see the right one was slightly swollen. He packed ice wraps around it, to keep the swelling down.

"It doesn't seem to be broken, but it'll take an x ray to be sure."

He wanted to ask so many questions, but she was clearly shaken, and her fear was real. Until he or they knew more, though, he couldn't do anything about that. Instead, he took her hand in one of his, leaned on an elbow to stroke her hair back with the other. It was against protocol, but he didn't care, it was obvious she needed gentleness right now. Solace. Her eyes closed and her expression eased at his touch.

Then she turned her cheek into his hand for comfort and he was lost.

# Chapter Five

The dog was a huge hit with Caleb's team, leaping up into the ARV to sniff around the vehicle and everyone in it. Watching them all warily. He was a handsome animal, with his black face and lean powerful body. And curious. Once he was properly introduced and Caleb was belted in, Ranger appropriated as much of Caleb's lap into which he could fit. To the amusement of the team. Not that Caleb minded much, ruffling the dog's fur.

"Okay, people, I don't know what's going on, yet, but it's clear those men were after the girl for whatever reason. Until we know more, we're on protection detail."

Ceili had said they were ex-military, which he knew by their actions, and/or mercenaries.

Why then were they after her? As pretty as she was, and she was that, she seemed like a normal woman, not the kind to attract that kind of attention. What the hell was going on?

Bear, who'd developed a fondness for the dog, volunteered to watch him and the entrance to the ER.

Detailing the rest of his people, Caleb strode into the hospital with Jax, their gear and badges giving them access to the ER.

Justin leaned against a wall, waiting. His eyebrows lifted in surprise to see Jax with them, although he clapped the other man on the arm in welcome.

"The doc is just finishing up," Justin said as he fell in alongside them. "Probably a concussion and a sprain of her ankle. Not enough to keep her here." He sounded worried. "With the concussion someone will need to keep an eye on her, though. And where is she going to go, now?"

"Let's get some answers first," Caleb said. "Then we'll figure the rest out. Shouldn't you be back on duty?"

Justin shrugged. "I called in a few favors, got someone to fill in my shift while we find out what's going on." He grinned wryly. "She keeps falling into my lap. Maybe someone or something is trying to tell me something."

Eyeing his brother, Caleb suspected there was more to it, but he didn't say anything.

A doctor was stepping out of one of the rooms as they walked down past other exam rooms. As they passed those other rooms, they could hear moaning or the murmur of voices. The doctor nodded to Justin, then eyed Caleb and Jax. "She's all yours."

Without Caleb having to say it, Jax took up position outside the door, apparently casually but watchful.

Giving Caleb a look, Justin pushed the door to the room they'd put Ceili in open and let Caleb inside first.

Even without makeup she still caught Caleb's attention with that neat tumble of golden-red hair framing her pretty face and those brilliant blue eyes. The dusting of golden freckles across her nose and cheeks was almost innocently charming.

She looked at them, at him, as they entered. Her gaze was open, direct, and intelligent, but he could see an undercurrent of something in the shadows that darkened those bright blue eyes.

"Justin," she said, "how's that officer? Will he be okay? Please tell me he'll be okay."

Taking a breath, Justin said, "One of the bullets hit his vest, two others hit him in the shoulder and arm. He's in surgery right now, but the doctors say his prognosis is good, provided there's no surprises."

She let her head fall back, closing her eyes and then let out a sigh of relief.

Caleb was surprised. That she was so worried about the injured officer said a lot about her.

He'd run the standard checks on her, no wants or warrants, no red flags except she had a bit of a lead foot. A trait they shared. She was, by all appearances, perfectly normal.

"Miss Whelan," he said, trying to keep his distance, keep it professional.

She looked at him, clearly a little surprised by the formality, and her lips curved in amusement. She lifted an eyebrow, rolled her eyes at him and shook her head – carefully – before tilting it a little to give him an assessing look.

"Caleb, I've kissed both your brothers and almost literally fallen at your feet, I think you can call me Ceili," she said. "Or I'll start calling you…" She turned to Justin, tipped her head a little at Caleb and stage-whispered conspiratorially, "Does he have a title?" Those pretty blue eyes twinkled with mischief.

Smothering a grin, Justin started to answer.

"All right, all right," Caleb conceded, somewhat amused. "Ceili, it is."

Pulling up the only chair he spun it around so he could straddle it.

"So," he said, "do you want to tell me what's going on? Why were those men after you?"

Her smile vanished as if it had never been and that pierced him. He found he was sorry to see it go. And that he was the reason why it did. The question had to be asked, though. It was why he was here. He needed to know what the hell was going on.

Taking a long slow breath, she turned carefully to sit up cross-legged on the bed to face him, drawing up a bit of the sheet. Her fingers worried at it.

"Believe it or not, it's because I tried to do the right thing." She sighed and paused, looking down at her hands as they moved restlessly, before looking back up at him and Justin. "The law of unintended consequences. You know there's been a huge explosion of drug use and abuse, especially opioids, and synthetic opioids like fentanyl."

Justin nodded. "We carry naloxone for both addicts and accidental exposure by emergency personnel."

She nodded.

"I was a researcher for the state, and I was good at it. I'm endlessly curious and I like solving puzzles. They knew a lot of drugs were passing through the hands of doctors, many by prescription, one of the most common ways to get hooked on opioids. Some doctors and pharmacists saw or were offered the opportunity for an easy way to make money. Suppliers said to them, write this script for this patient, or fill it, and we'll pay you for each. And suppliers were only too glad to provide. Addicts would go from doctor to doctor, pharmacist to pharmacist. That was the semi-legal side. If some of it wandered, it wasn't their fault. Except in some cases, it was. Some didn't care. And some were just dealers, opiates, heroin, cocaine, and the synthetics. Some combined them to lethal effect in many cases or added it to marijuana in states where there's no regulations.

They needed to shut the pipelines down.

So the state asked me to look, to find the sources, who was ordering too much, who was supplying too much. Just research, finding a paper trail. Like with Capone and his taxes. Following the money. Who was getting too rich from what was supposed to be legal distribution.

I had family and friends who'd lost people they loved to the epidemic whether to addiction or death, so I was more than glad to help. The state investigators knew doctors, pharmacists, pharmaceutical suppliers and so on were involved, first by dispensing them, and then as their patients became addicted, becoming their dealers. The state gave me nearly unlimited access and I started looking for the connections, the drug suppliers, doctors, pharmacists. Who was overprescribing. Who were providing the drugs they were dispensing? The more I looked the more I found. But there were one or two who seemed more involved than the others, so I looked harder and deeper at them."

Raising her eyes to Caleb, to Justin, she looked abashed.

"It became an obsession. The statistics were horrifying, it ate at me. Hundreds die across the country every day. I couldn't stop. I was reporting what I was finding, and that got federal investigators involved, especially when I could show them the proof they'd been looking for. They'd been after a specific target, but they couldn't find the hard evidence. It was like the pieces of a puzzle, this piece to this piece to this piece. I just put the puzzle pieces together. A lot of what Janssen was doing was legal, cover for his illegal activities. I tied it all together. It was enough. They convened a grand jury to seek an indictment and asked me to testify about what I'd found. They were closing in on him. Some of the other information that came out during the trial was how Janssen used ex-military and mercenaries as enforcers, assassins, both here and overseas. Including against law enforcement. He was raking the money in. Millions. All by computers. One of his couriers was carrying a fortune in blood diamonds when he crashed his car. Janssen was selling drugs around the world."

"Even though I was the key witness, the one who had put it together, I wasn't worried, after all I was just a researcher, a desk jockey."

"They issued warrants, started taking some people down. But not the spider at the center. Somehow Janssen learned they were onto him, was tipped off either by one of his associates or a government employee, so he escaped to somewhere in the Far East, the Philippines, Indonesia, Thailand, someplace like them. Places where the US had no extradition treaties."

"No one," she said, "not even me, expected him to go after me. It made no sense. The prosecutors, the grand jury, had all my research, that couldn't be changed or undone. And I was just a researcher. No threat."

She took a shuddering breath. Her hand rose to her nose, to the little bump there. She flinched, her eyes went bleak and haunted. "But he did."

"The first time came out of the blue," she said. "I'd been out for drinks with friends. As I walked to my car I suddenly was surrounded. Street thugs. One of them said something about Janssen and then he hit me. It seemed like my head exploded. I tried to fight, but I couldn't stop them. It was luck that one of the people waiting to get into the club I'd just left saw what was happening, started shouting, and called 911. Everyone, even the cops, chalked it up to a woman walking alone at night."

Listening, seeing the expression in her eyes, remembering what she'd said on the way to the hospital, was more than Justin could take. He sat on the bed and gathered her into his lap.

To feel his strong arms around her was an incredible relief. She pressed her cheek against his chest, closed her eyes and for a moment simply breathed him in as she listened to the steady beat of his heart.

Justin cradled her head.

His kindness, his comfort, was a balm to battered nerves and body but she had to finish. She took a long slow breath.

Caleb saw her shoulders straighten and then she looked at him. He thought he'd drown in those blue eyes, in the pain and fear in them, the courage, and the despair.

"It didn't stop. They tried to run my car off the road."
She smiled, suddenly fierce. "They chose the wrong road and
the wrong driver. My little car could kick ass and drift
corners. They hadn't expected that."

He had to admire that sudden shift of mood. "I've seen
your records."

"Uh oh," she said, then added, affronted. "They were
going to put me in jail. For speeding. On a highway."

"Three tickets in less than six months," he commented,
glad to see her mood lighten again. It seemed to be more her
nature. "Judges can only tolerate so much. You're a speed
demon."

She eyed him, eyes sparkling. "I am. Going to arrest me,
officer?" she asked, holding her wrists out to him.

The mental image of her in handcuffs, with that impish
grin, took his thoughts in an entirely inappropriate direction.
His body, though, thought differently. He was suddenly, but
not unpleasantly, a little uncomfortable, aroused as his
imagination ran riot. It was a bit of a surprise to him to find
he was as attracted to her as his brothers. Or maybe not so
much of a surprise – they were brothers.

With an effort, he reined himself in.

Oblivious, she continued, "They broke into my
apartment. That was the last straw. The police responded but
that was all. It wasn't proof I needed protection. It just
seemed like a home invasion. The prosecutors had already
moved on. I wasn't part of an active case anymore. Not that
they didn't want to, but they had nothing for them to point at
and say, 'she's in danger' that didn't have a more common
explanation. Wedged behind the refrigerator I'd heard the
men who broke in talking. Janssen wanted payback. I knew it
wasn't over. So, I packed up everything and ran. I researched
the best ways to go into hiding, used my charge card to get
cash to pay bills so there'd be no record of the location of the

final transaction. Searched for another job, used the income from that, keeping my old account in reserve, transferring money out in small amounts. It bought me time."

"That's why you got Ranger," Caleb said.

She nodded, her mouth quirking. "I was hoping I'd lost them, but I wasn't taking any chances. So, I got Ranger. We trained together from when Ranger was no longer a puppy, but not quite a dog. He was about six months old or so. The trainer was ex-military himself. When I told him my story, I'm not sure he completely believed me, but he taught me some basic self-defense, too."

Remembering Tom and his wife Annie made her heart ache. They'd semi-adopted her, given her a home away from her tiny apartment. Until the next attack. Ranger's training, never tested until that moment, held. But it also showed her that people she knew and loved were at risk, simply for being too close.

Once more, she'd been forced to run.

A nurse opened the door to poke her head in. "If you're through here, we need this room. We have patients waiting."

Reality crashed over Ceili. Where could she go? She still had no money. She wouldn't have replacement cards for a few days. With no address she'd had to have them sent to the bank and she had no cash. She had the bus pass and what little money was left on the card the Red Cross had given her.

And she couldn't leave Ranger.

"What will you do now?" Caleb asked. "You clearly need protection. Where will you go, in case we need to contact you?"

She'd been asking herself the same question. Her heart sank. She had no alternatives. It was hardly the first time she'd wound up on the street.

"I have my cell phone, you can always reach me on it. It's been charged. Otherwise, I just need to pick up Ranger.

Someone can drop us off at a bus station or we can walk," she said. It wouldn't be the first time they'd slept in one, she and Ranger. Or on a bench at a bus stop. "Tomorrow I can go to a library, use their computers, see if I can get an advance on my pay to carry me until my new charge cards arrive."

A bus station.

Justin looked at Caleb, shaking his head.

"Like hell," Justin said firmly, his eyes locked on Caleb's almost in defiance. "We've got room at our place."

Although Caleb understood his brother's anger and frustration, it wasn't necessary, Caleb had no intention of leaving her on the street. Nor could his people protect her there. She'd been through enough. He didn't have the budget or okay from the powers on high to provide a safe house, but he wasn't going to leave her at another impersonal hotel or motel when they themselves had the room.

What neither of them expected was an objection from her.

"No," she said, and tried to escape Justin's lap. "No."

She looked at them both as Justin held her firmly in place.

"They know I'm here, in this city. I can't, I won't, put either of you or Jesse at risk."

"I can take care of myself," Justin said.

Raising a hand to his face, her fingers tracing his cheekbone, Ceili looked into his amber eyes. "It's not that, Justin, but… if anything happened to any of you, because of me..." Her eyes went bright. She shook her head. "Like that officer. Or worse."

Caleb eyed her, crossing his arms. "You do know I'm with SWAT. I also served a couple of tours overseas, Special Forces, in Iraq and Afghanistan."

"They never come alone, you're one man. You had a team at the motel."

Reasonably he said, "I still have a team." He tipped his head at his brother. "There's my brothers. Both were deployed overseas as well. We have the room. You need a place to stay. With no records to track, they won't know where you are."

Those eyes lifted to his, her lips parted. She looked stunned and so vulnerable. It was clear she'd given up even daring to hope, and yet she still found humor in life. He remembered a line from an old movie. She… abided. Survived. Fought. He remembered her clinging to the railing, sliding beneath it. Her fingers slipping. She fought and kept fighting.

"I can't…" Her breath came short, caught, remembering Tom. The car windows exploding. She closed her eyes. "It's too much to ask. I can't."

"How long?" he asked. "How long have you been running?"

She bowed her head, but he saw the tears appear on her lashes even as she fought them back. She shook her head. "Not so long. A few years. Sooner or later, they'll give up. They have to." It was all she dared hope.

Years. Just the thought pained Caleb.

"And how are you going to manage Ranger on crutches?" he asked. "Tonight, though…"

He looked to his brother. Justin nodded.

"You stay with us. No better safe house. We'll take it day by day until we can figure out what to do."

# Chapter Six

Having just come off shift after getting his notes logged into the computer, Jesse had only been home for a few minutes when to his surprise the door opened. Justin and Caleb were both supposed to be on shift. He was startled to see Ranger bound in. The dog took one look at him and barked happily. He planted his feet on Jesse's chest to give his chin a lick, stopped for a moment for a ruffle of his ears and then he raced around the condo to smell everything.

Bemused, he looked toward the door as Justin followed the dog inside, with Ceili beside him on crutches.

"What the hell?" he said, looking from his twin to Ceili.

"Long story, Jess," Justin said, with a tip of his head at Ceili. "It's been a rough night so we're putting Ceili up."

"It must have been," he said, eyeing the crutches.

"Ceili can have my room, I'll take the couch."

Eyeing the length of him and then the couch, Ceili gave him a look. "Justin, I'm not going to kick you out of your own bed and besides you won't fit on that."

He grinned. "It wouldn't be the first time I've slept there." Although he'd had a few kinks in his neck and knees when he woke.

"That may be, but I'm still not going to kick you out of your own bed. I'll take the couch. It's more my size." Suddenly she went still. "It's too quiet. Where's Ranger? Damn, I can't take my eyes off that dog for a second. Ranger!"

Ranger raced down the stairs, a leather slipper in his mouth. He'd clearly been chewing on it. The laces were gone, and some of the sheepskin lining had been torn out.

"Please don't tell me that's one of Caleb's," she said, looking at them with a plea in her eyes.

Smothering a grin, Jesse said, "Then we won't." Although it was. Caleb rarely wore them, though.

"Ranger, give."

He didn't, instead backing away, shaking his head and the slipper vigorously, ready to play.

Laughing, Jesse said, "We'll never get it away from him now."

"I'm afraid you're right," she said, ruefully, running her hand through her hair. Her fingers snagged at the back of her head. "Would you mind if I borrowed your shower? I desperately need to get my hair clean."

She tried not to look at Jesse when she said it, remembering the last time she'd expressed a need for a shower – and that kiss. Warmth curled low in her belly. But there was Justin, too. The memory of kissing him was just as vivid. She liked them both too much.

"That might make Ranger curious enough to rescue the slipper," she said, trying to keep herself distracted from thoughts of these two handsome men. Not just brothers, but twins. She didn't know how they felt, and she couldn't pick one over the other. Wouldn't. And she wouldn't play games with them, with their heads, they didn't deserve that.

"We'll get some blankets for the couch while you do that," Justin said, with a glance at Jesse. His brother had seen the slight blush, too, and noticed she wouldn't look either of them in the eye. Something sparked in his brother's eyes, a touch of curiosity, as well as attraction. Justin knew she'd kissed them both. And he remembered kissing her, a hungry need firing between them, and his mind wandered in interesting directions. Since she wouldn't look at either of them, she was clearly caught between them. That thought brought up another, the image of Ceili sandwiched between him and his brother. A shot of heat went through him.

She shook her finger at him. "I'm not taking your bed, Justin Armitage, so don't even try. The couch will do just fine."

He grinned, holding up his hands. "I wouldn't dream of it."

But the thought of her in his bed didn't help.

Jesse said, "Leave what you're wearing in the bathroom, you can wash them in the morning, I have an old tee you can use for tonight."

"That would be wonderful," Ceili said, gratefully, and then looked at the stairs, realizing she'd need to get up them on crutches.

"I got this," Jesse said, seeing where her eyes went.

The next thing Ceili knew Jesse swept her up in his arms as easily as if she weighed nothing. She was suddenly and sharply aware of the muscles clearly on display beneath his tee shirt and in his arms beneath her back and her legs. Behind him came Justin. They were going to make her crazy.

Ranger trotted ahead of them keeping just out of arm's reach, the slipper still in his mouth. Hopeful for a game.

"Silly dog," she said.

His eyes brightened and his ears perked up. She shook her head at him. He didn't care, he just wanted someone to play with.

Jesse carried her into the bathroom, setting her down just outside the shower.

"Can you keep her steady, Jess, while I get the wrapping off her ankle?" Justin asked.

"Got her," Jesse said, curling an arm around her waist.

Ceili steadied herself with hand on Jesse's arm, far too aware of him so close and the sheer power in the arm beneath her hand. Just as she was aware of Justin going to one knee in front of her, his fingers gentle as he unwound the bandage from around her ankle. Even with Jesse's arm around her, his hand just beneath her breast, she wanted to reach out to run her fingers through Justin's silky dark hair. She fought the urge, even when he glanced up at her with those golden eyes.

"Be careful, the tiles can be slippery," Justin said, unconsciously running his hand up her leg, over the firm muscle of her calf, all too aware of the feel of her soft skin beneath his fingers.

Swallowing hard, Ceili nodded.

Her blue eyes softened, as did her mouth, when their eyes met. His cock, already hardening, came to sudden attention, even with his brother's arm around her. Or maybe because of…

He took a deep breath.

Even to his own ears, his voice was rough as he looked at his brother. "I'll get the blankets."

"And close all the doors to rooms you don't want Ranger to go in," she said, and he was gratified to hear her voice sounded a little unsteady, too.

Jesse released her carefully, keeping a hand close until he was sure she had hers on the railing that ran around the inside of the shower. He'd been very aware of her body against his, and how close she was. "Do you have it?"

Looking up at him, she took a breath and nodded.

He fought the urge to join her there, but before he did anything, he needed to know how Justin felt, how he wanted to or was handling this. Because he knew his brother well enough to see the signs that he was just as attracted to Ceili as he was himself. How *were* they going to handle this? Unlike some of the women they'd dealt with in the past, Ceili didn't show a preference for one over the other, or mess with one of them while looking at the other, but something told him she was just as drawn to them as they were to her.

Reluctantly, he let her go. "I'll get that tee for you."

He leaned in to turn on the tap so the water would be hot when she got in.

"Thank you," she said softly.

"Yell if you need anything."

"I will," she promised. "Leave the bathroom door open a crack for Ranger, would you? Otherwise he'll claw up the door trying to get in."

"Knowing that dog? Yeah, I'll do that," he said, shaking his head with a grin.

A part of her didn't want him to go, but a part of her did. The attraction she felt for both him and his brother had her head spinning and she couldn't choose. They were each unique, Justin gentle, Jesse fierce. And she was just as attracted to Caleb, if for different reasons. His sureness, those dark, piercing eyes, that sexy mouth. What would it be like to kiss that mouth, to kiss him?

This had to stop, she needed to get control of herself, she told herself. Unsuccessfully.

She leaned her head against the cool frosted, pebbled glass of the shower for just a moment, trying to gather her wits around her. They were sweet torture, and she wanted… each of them, all of them, nearly unbearably. And that wasn't possible. Couldn't be possible. Not that she was even sure they wanted her as much as she did them.

It was an act of will to strip out of her clothes and step into the shower, but then the soothing heat of the water hit her neck and shoulders. Muscles she hadn't known were sore and tight, loosened. With one arm on the rail, she turned around, letting her head fall back to let the water stream over her hair, and her overstretched neck, shoulders and back.

That was the image of her Jesse saw when he stepped into the bathroom to give her the tee, the silhouette of her body through the frosted glass, and he went hard again in an instant.

One of her arms was raised so she could run her fingers through her hair while she steadied herself with the other. Her back was arched, lifting her full breasts high. He was frozen for a moment, locked on the sight of her. Imagining her with water running over that lovely body. It was an incredibly erotic image, and completely inadvertent on her part. She didn't even know he was there. Beneath his sweatpants his shaft went rigid and as hard as a rock. It was an effort not to strip out of the sweatpants and join her in there, to run his hands over her wet body. He willed himself strength, took a slow deep breath, hung the tee beside the towel on the bar and left before she saw him.

Damn, but the woman was going to kill him. He went down to help Justin get the couch ready.

Ceili reveled in the feel of the warm water, the spicy scent of their shampoo in her hair as she scrubbed at it, getting all the blood and dirt out. It stung where the gun had hit her and she winced, but she was too grateful to be clean again.

Hobbling out of the shower, she was grateful to see Jesse's promised tee shirt beside the towel. She toweled off, then tugged the tee shirt over her head. Thankfully he was so much taller it was long enough to cover the fact she wasn't wearing underwear, and it was so well-worn the cotton was wonderfully soft. It was, however, one of those muscle tee shirts, strappy and v-necked or so well worn it was nearly the same thing. She was just grateful to be wearing something clean she didn't care how it looked.

Ranger, as expected, was stretched out on the rug by the sink.

She found that as long as she didn't put her whole weight on her ankle and braced herself against the wall, she could walk after a fashion. She wasn't certain she could handle being carried again – and it would be harder to hide that she wasn't wearing underwear. Besides, she didn't want to take advantage of them more than was necessary. She would do as much for herself as she could. Unfortunately, in that Ranger couldn't help, he just wasn't quite tall enough for her to lean on. She made it to the stairs, and then she had the railing for support.

That was the sight that greeted Caleb at the sound of someone on the stairs – Ceili, dressed in a t-shirt so old and worn it draped over every curve, dipped deeply between her full breasts. The cotton was so thin it was nearly transparent, her areola slightly darker shadows against it. Her nipples tented the material. Her hair gleamed like the sunset in the lights. In an instant his body went hard and tight. So did his cock.

A glance at his brothers showed them equally as transfixed.

It was a good thing she was concentrating on getting down the stairs, completely unaware of the effect she was having on them. Then Ranger bounded forward, breaking the spell, and her eyes lifted to meet his.

He saw her breath catch, her eyes warm at the sight of him and then she smiled.

"Caleb, you're home!"

Her clear delight at seeing him pleased him more than he was willing to admit, even to himself.

"Ceili," Justin chided, "one of us would have come to help."

She looked at him. "I don't want to be a problem when I can do it myself."

"You're not," Jesse said.

Tugging the tee shirt down, Ceili warned, "Don't you dare pick me up, Jesse, or your brothers will get an eyeful."

It was an idea none of them seemed to mind. She tried very hard to pretend she hadn't noticed.

The yawn caught her off-guard.

Jesse swept her off her feet. "They'll just have to take their chances. It's late, and it's been a long day for all of us."

He deposited her on the couch where he and Justin had spread a sheet, blankets, and a pillow for her. "Bed, you."

It was as if the whole day crashed down on her shoulders as a wave of exhaustion washed through her. She clapped a hand over her mouth to hide another yawn.

"I'm so sorry."

"Don't be," he said and kissed her forehead. "It's no wonder you're tired. I'm surprised you lasted this long."

She looked up at him, the sweet gesture so unexpected, then at each of them.

"Thank you for this," she said, her voice soft.

Justin brushed a hand over her hair as he went by. "Our pleasure, Ceili. Time for all of us to grab a few zzzz's. Sweet dreams, sweetheart."

She smiled at him, her eyelids already nearly at half-mast. Once more, she fought back a yawn.

"Down," Jesse said.

Ranger sat.

That got a chuckle out of all of them.

Laughing, Jesse said, "I meant your boss, dog." He turned to Ceili. "I said down."

She arched a brow at him. "Do I look like a dog?" She looked at Justin and Caleb. "Bossy, isn't he?"

"No, you definitely don't look like a dog. But if you think he's bad?" Justin said and jerked a thumb at Caleb. "Wait until he gets into it."

A yawn caught her mid-grin.

"See," Jesse said.

"Go to sleep, sweetheart," Justin said.

Grinning but obedient, Ceili stretched out on the couch, tugging the covers over her as she closed her eyes.

"As long as you don't expect me to wag my tail," she said, as she curled up around her pillow. She glanced over her shoulder at them with sleepy eyes, and then did just that, beneath the blankets.

Caleb was enjoying the interplay, but that was almost too much for him. He closed his eyes and swallowed a groan.

Giving Jesse a look, Justin said, "Payback is a bitch."

"I heard that," she said, and blew raspberries at him.

He laughed.

"Goodnight," she murmured. "Sweet dreams."

Both his brothers turned for the stairs, but Caleb lingered a moment at the bottom, just to look.

Exhausted, she'd fallen asleep nearly instantly, one hand curled beneath her cheek, her brilliant hair tousled, looking oddly innocent. He tried to banish the image of her in that tee out of his mind as he followed his brothers up the stairs but found he couldn't.

Out of habit, he shut off the lights as he went.

"Does one of you want to tell me what happened tonight," Jesse said, quietly. He'd seen the blood matting Ceili's hair before she'd showered. "And who I have to kill?"

Even the condensed version took some telling.

"What are we going to do about it?" Jesse asked when they were finished, his eyes going from Caleb to his twin.

Justin said, "Which it? That we all want her or the trouble she's in?"

"Either. Both." Jesse let out a breath.

Caleb kept his thoughts on the first to himself.

He'd been through the relationship wars more times than he could count. For that matter, so had his brothers. He'd even married, sure that he'd found the 'one'. Alison had had other ideas. Fidelity was not her long suit.

Ceili, though, in the few hours he'd known her, from the reports on the fire, the statements of her neighbors, and all his brothers had said, had already proven herself to be ten times the woman he'd thought Alison was. The risk she'd taken to go back into that building, suspecting it was on fire. She was stronger than she knew or would give herself credit for, yet tender and caring enough that her neighbors spoke highly of her. And points to her for treading the line with Justin and Jesse. He'd noted that she tried to keep distance between herself and them, rather than playing one against the other despite being clearly attracted to both, it was his brothers who couldn't. If she couldn't choose, she wouldn't. She was intelligent and funny. Despite everything she was going through she found humor in things still.

Was he attracted to her? Yes. Far too much. In a few short hours she'd gotten under his skin. She drew him with her combination of strength and fragility, her courage. She was pretty in her own unique way with that tumbled mop of wavy, golden-red hair, those brilliant, direct blue eyes, and lush curves. Seeing her in that tee shirt had made him want to cup one full breast, brush his thumb over her nipple to feel it tighten, run his other hand over the firm curve of her ass to pull her against him. Just the thought made his cock stiffen.

Caleb remembered the warmth in her eyes and smile when she'd greeted him. She'd been genuinely glad to see him.

He couldn't deny the first, but the other? "On the last, I don't know, yet. I need to know more about what happened, and who this Janssen is. Once I do, maybe we can figure out a way to help her."

He was still mulling it over as he went down to his own bedroom, stripping out of his clothes.

A small sound from downstairs, though, and Ranger's whine, caught his attention. He grabbed a pair of old sweatpants and tugged them on. Something was wrong.

*****

Darkness, and someone or something in the darkness was closing in on her. Ceili sensed someone was there, she could feel it as she had the night her apartment had been broken into, but it was so dark she couldn't see whoever or whatever it was any more than she could that night. He or it was coming for her. Terror shot her out of sleep, the nightmare more vivid than reality. Gasping, heart hammering, she tried to stifle the betraying sounds escaping her as she tumbled off the couch, scrambled for a safe corner. Pain lanced through her ankle. Only half awake, all she knew was the darkness of the room and those dark figures, somewhere in the house. How close? Where could she hide?

Fear had her heart pounding.

Reaching the corner, she backed into it, her hand in Ranger's fur. He whined.

It was a dream, only a dream, awareness of that, knowing she'd had dreams like it before, didn't help. Terror still raced through her. She braced herself, tried to will herself to calm. Struggled to breathe more evenly, more steadily.

Where was she? For a moment she couldn't remember, and the darkness didn't help. Fear tried to close around her again.

The light on the stairs came on, and the events of the night all came rushing back to her, mixed with the memories of other times.

Ceili closed her eyes, fighting panic. It was a dream, she knew it had only been a dream. In memory she heard bullets and glass shattering. She tried to stifle the cry that escaped her.

She looked up to see Caleb standing there, his eyes sharp, focused on her, his long lean body bare but for a pair of sweatpants clinging to his hips. Even through the fear she was conscious of the beauty of him, his strong, fine features, the intensity of his dark eyes, the strength in his long lean body, in the curve of the muscles of his chest, the ripple of his abs, each clearly defined. But her memories and the nightmare still held her.

Huddled against the wall, she closed her eyes, pressed her hand to her mouth as her eyes burned. She held the tears back by sheer will.

One look at her, at the panic and fear in Ceili's expression, and Caleb knew. After all she'd been through, the attacks, the terror of them, for all those years, Ceili had post-traumatic stress disorder. A nightmare had her tight in its grip. He and his brothers had fought through them and sometimes still did. But they also had each other's backs, stood for each other when the dreams and memories came back to torment them. She didn't. For years she'd fought a war, alone.

He was moving before he even thought about it, gathering her up in his arms to carry her back to the couch. Fighting for control, struggling against the memories, she trembled, straining against him as she tried to rein in her fear. To conquer the instinct of flight or fight. He banded an arm around her, held her close, stroked her hair.

"You're safe," he said, repeated it, keeping his voice soft.

Ceili felt the strength of his arms around her, his long, lean body against hers. She desperately needed that comfort, needed something to hold on to, to anchor her against the fear.

It had been so long since anyone had held her like this, touched her. So long since she had dared let anyone close enough. But the one holding her was strong, sure Caleb. That was real, he was real, wasn't he? She needed to know. Needed to be sure. Needed to touch.

Those blue eyes looked up at Caleb, her gaze locked on his. Her firm mouth softened as her trembling fingers traced his cheekbone, finding reality in that delicate touch. Almost in wonder, she ran her fingers ever so lightly over his mouth. She closed her eyes a moment and let out a sigh, before looking up at him again. Her fingers hadn't stopped moving, trailing down to his chest, to slip over him in a delicate caress. His body went taut as her fingertips drifted. She was completely focused on that touch. On touching him. On the reality of him.

Her wandering fingers tested his control, yet he couldn't bring himself to ask her to stop. Not just for her own need but, suddenly, for his own. Her eyes rose to look into his as her lips parted on a sigh, and he was suddenly very aware the weight of her in his lap. Of her body against his, of her full breast beneath the thin cotton pressed against his chest. He was as hard as a rock beneath her.

Control snapped.

In the next moment his mouth was on hers. He speared his fingers into the soft waves of her hair to draw her mouth hard against his to devour her. Her lips parted as she gasped in surprise. And more, need. It was an invitation. One he took. The taste of her was so clean, so fresh and sweet. Cradling her head, he eased her down to the couch as he stretched out next to her, his mouth still on hers. He needed, wanted. She responded with her own need, her own want.

She turned into him, wrapped a leg around his, to press every inch of her body tight against his.

The fingers of one hand speared deep into his hair as the other circled his shoulders. A soft sound escaped her as she tightened her arms around him.

"Caleb," she whispered.

Him. What she wanted was him. As he wanted her. Badly.

Caleb ran his hand down the slender column of her throat, skimmed it over her fullness beneath the thin cotton. Her back arched to press her breast against his palm, the nipple hardening. He ran his hand down over her ribs and groaned as her abs tightened in response. Down further, past the thin tee shirt to slide between her thighs. She gasped as he cupped her mound, to find her damp. Her hips rose and her thighs parted, opened to him.

He needed to see her, all of her. Grasping the hem of the tee, he stripped it over her head, tossed it away, and she was bared to him. For a moment all he could do was look at her. God, she was beautiful. All those sweet lush curves. He stroked a hand over one full, firm breast, the nipple now hard against his palm. Curling his fingers around her breast, he cupped it, raised it so he could taste her. He sucked that tender pink tip into his mouth as she gasped, her back bowing to offer him more.

A small sound on the stairs caught his attention.

Raising his head, he found his brothers watching. Both clearly aroused.

That was all Caleb needed to see.

"Ceili had a nightmare," he said as she turned her head and started with surprise to see Jesse and Justin standing there. "I could use some help."

She gasped, her eyes going to each of them as they slid her to the plush carpet.

Caleb didn't give her time to think. He cupped a breast, ran his thumb over her hardening nipple. A soft moan escaped her as she trembled.

Jesse looked at his twin. At the sight of Ceili naked, her lush firm curves bared to them as Caleb played with her, fire had flared within him. It was incredibly erotic to watch. Justin clearly felt the same. They'd both wanted her, and so had Caleb. Watching him play with her, at her eyes widen at the sight of them, now they knew they could have her, too, all of them as Caleb offered her breast to them.

That was an invitation Jesse couldn't pass up. Stretching out beside them, beside her, Jesse sucked on the tender tip, and her back arched to offer him more. And he took what was offered, gladly, sucking as much of her into his mouth as he could, and then suckling on that rosy flesh hard. She moaned.

Caleb slid his hand down over her flat belly to cup her mound again for both their pleasure. Her breath caught as he slid his fingers over the delicate tissues between her thighs and then slid two of them inside her. Her breath shuddered. She was more than damp now, and his blood went hot. He stroked his fingers deep, then slid them out to tease her clit.

A hand stroked Ceili's hair as Caleb's fingers teased her and Jesse devoured her breast. She looked up to see Justin as his mouth lowered to hers.

"God, I want you, Ceili," Justin said, before claiming her mouth.

"We all do," Jesse said.

Ceili hadn't known what to feel when she'd seen them standing there, guilt warring with need and desire in her. They were each so different, each so handsome, so beautiful in body. Jesse's muscles so strongly curved, Justin's defined like Caleb's.

Then Justin's mouth found hers as Jesse shifted down her body. Justin's fingers toyed with her nipple, and there was only them, only her desire for them.

One of Caleb's legs twined with hers to draw it back, opening her to them. She cried out as Caleb's mouth found her breast again to suckle and nibble. Each nip sent a shot of heat down to her core.

Hands pressed her thighs gently, urging them further apart. Jesse. His fingers exposed her clit. A warm mouth covered it, surrounded it. His tongue touched her, explored her, danced, slipped and slid around her delicate nub and heat rushed through her. It swirled low in her belly in rhythm to his sweet torment. She opened to him, to them, to offer them more. All thought, all memories, vanished before their erotic assault on her senses. She couldn't think, didn't want to, all she wanted to do was feel. All she wanted was them.

Justin draped her arm across his shoulders as his mouth closed on her other breast to suck, nip and nibble.

With his hand on her abs to feel her body arch, her hips rise, Caleb did the same, each tremble and quiver a promise of what was to come. As his brothers kept her attention, he pushed the loose sweatpants off, kicked them away. Now it was only her skin against his, as she shifted and moved against him. The motion of her body teased his already throbbing cock.

Licking and lapping, suckling, Jesse toyed with that small, tender nub, each quiver a reward. He slid two fingers inside her, curled them a little, pumping them slowly into her. He gently finger-fucked her as he licked and sucked at her clit until her hips rose and fell in response to each motion of his mouth, each stroke of his fingers. Her head tossed restlessly, her eyes blind to everything but them.

Pleasure rushed through Ceili at Caleb and Justin's mouths suckling on her nipples and each sweet touch of

Jesse's tongue on her clit. She could no longer think, only surrender to what they did to her. Wave after wave of sheer bliss drove her higher, her body going taut, quivering, bowed, balanced on the very edge of ecstasy.

She wasn't aware of each moan and gasp that escaped her, the soft cry that was wrenched from her when Jesse briefly sucked a little harder. Pleasure shot through her, pooled low within her. She was delirious with it, with them. It was maddening, she was so close, so close. She needed. She couldn't hold still except where Jesse's hands clasped her hips, held them in place.

"Please," she said, her body quivering helplessly.

Caleb shifted.

She looked up to see him braced on an arm above her, sliding a condom over his shaft with the other, then stroking his rigid, twitching cock.

"Oh, God, Caleb, yes, please yes," she gasped. She needed to be filled, to have one of them inside her.

In the next moment Jesse sucked, hard, at her clit. She cried out as she came, as ecstasy exploded through her. Then Jesse was gone. She looked up to see Caleb above her, his eyes dark and intent, and then his cock slammed into her to drive another cry from her. And again, pounding deep inside her. Her hips bucked, demanding more, harder… and he gave it to her, hammering into her as she cried out with each hard, relentless stroke.

She was so tight around Caleb's throbbing length, so warm and damp. She felt incredible as her pleasure closed around his rigid shaft. Her orgasm gloved and stroked him as her legs wrapped around his to take him deeper still, her hips thrusting against his. It was incredible, her body quivering, trembling inside and out as he took her. Her orgasm pulsed around him, tight around him. She took him with her, and he came, hard and fast, his own ecstasy erupting inside her, his hips driving against her relentlessly, spurt after spurt, filling her as she bucked and thrust to take him, to take everything he gave her.

He collapsed over her.

Bowing his head, he leaned his forehead against hers for a moment before taking her mouth again, kissing her softly yet deeply before sliding away to make room for one of his brothers.

Ceili was utterly limp, but they gave her no respite.

Fingers stroked inside her, keeping her from relaxing completely, and then a mouth suckled at her clit while Caleb reclaimed her breast. Nibbling and suckling, Jesse had her hard and aching in moments as his talented mouth drove her wild once again. Her body trembled, quivered, at the command of his tongue, of his fingers stroking inside her.

"Ceili?"

Looking up, she saw Justin next to her, stroking his cock and knew what he wanted.

She licked her lips and heard him groan. Then she felt the broad head of his cock brush against her mouth. She flicked her tongue over her lips to taste his salty, musky pre-cum on them. He groaned. She looked up into his strong handsome face and then took the broad head of his shaft into her mouth, her tongue stroking over it, over him. Her eyes were on him, on his face, to see the pleasure she gave him, even as pleasure built inside her.

A deeper groan escaped him.

Both Caleb and Jesse looked up at the sound to see the head of Justin's cock slide between Ceili's pretty lips. Her arm went around his hips to draw him closer, deeper into her mouth.

Jesse watched his brother arch, his hand buried, clenched in Ceili's hair, his eyes closed with the pleasure of her mouth on him.

Judging by Caleb's expression it was one of the most erotic things either had ever seen.

At the sight, though, Jesse nearly lost it, his own cock so hard he nearly exploded his own pleasure over her abs. It was a near thing. He fought for control, and instead suckled at her clit, to make her moan around Justin's cock. His brother groaned in response and then she took him deeper while her back arched in response to Jesse's mouth on her. Her hips pumped, wanting, needing.

That was more than Jesse could take. He sucked hard on her clit, sending her flying even as he surged up her body to impale her on his own pulsing shaft, ramming it deep into her, hard and harder still as she closed around him. He pounded into her. She cried out around Justin's cock as her orgasm rocked her, her body tight around his shaft, and then his pleasure took him. His body arched, locked against hers as his hips pumped while she shook and trembled. He emptied into her, his cum pulsing inside her seemingly endlessly.

As much as Justin wanted to come inside that sweet mouth – and he would one day, he knew – he wanted to feel her pussy around him as Caleb and Jesse had.

He looked to his twin. Their eyes met.

Justin's cock pulled out of Ceili's mouth and she nearly cried out in protest, and then Jesse gave way to his twin and Justin rammed his shaft inside her still throbbing pussy, triggering an aftershock of pleasure so intense she did cry out. Her legs closed around his, pulled him tighter, harder against her.

Hearing her need, Justin gave it to her, slamming against her, driving into her, feeling the aftershock of her orgasm close tightly around him. He rode her hard, his hips slamming against hers, driving his shaft deep inside her, and she took him, all of him, her hips bucking against his. It was maddening, he couldn't take her hard enough. And then his own ecstasy erupted. His body was locked, rigid, as he emptied into her in wave after wave of pleasure.

They all collapsed to curl around Ceili, Caleb pulling the blankets after and over them, before drawing her tight against his side, her head on his shoulder, Justin on her other side, Jesse with his head pillowed just beneath her breasts.

Ceili was still trembling, but this time not from nightmares, this time from sheer pleasure. She'd never experienced anything like this. She felt delightfully limp and incredibly well-used.

In wonder, she reached out to Caleb to touch his face as she had earlier. This was real. They were real, and they had just fucked her nearly brainless. And it had been amazing.

Caleb caught her hand, turned his head to kiss her palm. That simple gesture sent an entirely different kind of warmth through her. She smiled at him, at all of them, stunned and amazed.

She stroked her hand through Jesse's hair as he kissed her belly, and then she turned her head to look at Justin. He kissed her gently.

"What just happened?" she asked, her voice the barest whisper.

Caleb answered. "I think we all just fucked you blind. And enjoyed the hell out of it."

"And want to do it again," Justin said. "God, you're so responsive, sweetheart. And your mouth…" He groaned. "That was incredible."

She blinked. "None of you mind?"

Jesse said, "We have cousins who have a similar arrangement. We just didn't think we'd find it ourselves, didn't even consider it to be honest. Then you appeared, sweet and tough, vulnerable, in trouble but determined. No, I certainly don't mind sharing you with my brothers. And Justin's right, you're responsive as all hell."

"None of us do," Caleb said. "And judging by your reaction, you don't either."

"I never even imagined this," she answered. "As long as you don't mind, I certainly don't. Do with me what you will. That was incredible."

"Be careful what you ask for," Caleb said, remembering an earlier thought and watching her pleasure his brother. So many possibilities…

Ranger came to join them, to lie against Caleb's back. The weight of the dog, light as he was, pushed him closer to Ceili. Something he couldn't mind at all.

But.

"We can't stay here, or we'll all wake up stiff in the morning."

With a grin, Justin said, curling closer to Ceili, his arm around her pulling her tighter against him, "Which we're likely to do anyway." His imagination was already wandering, wondering, considering.

She gave him a look, eyes twinkling.

Jesse was already scooping her up.

"Hey," Justin protested.

"Mom always told you to share your toys," Jesse asked, giving his twin a grin. "Your bedroom, Caleb?"

"Jesse, I'm not a toy," Ceili protested, amused.

"You are fun to play with," he said.

"My room, it's closest," Caleb answered.

# Chapter Seven

Ceili woke with three firmly muscled male bodies cuddled around her. The reality of it still boggled her mind, not that she was complaining. Not by a long shot. No demons of the past had disturbed her dreams for once or would dare to with these three around her.

An arm pulled her closer. Justin. Turning her head, she looked at him. He was still asleep, it was just instinct.

She smiled.

Jesse's head was pillowed on her stomach, his arm around her hips, his body stretched out between her legs. Her head rested on Caleb's shoulder, his arm cradling her neck, his other hand curled around her breast.

She sighed, sweetly content.

Nearby she could hear Ranger dreaming, soft woofs, his claws scrabbling against the carpet, his muscles undoubtedly twitching as he chased dream rabbits.

It didn't get much better than this. For the moment, she wouldn't question it, she'd just enjoy it.

She knew the longer she stayed, the more danger they would be in, over and above the dangers they faced every day. For whatever time she could, though, she'd just enjoy their company, their touch, and do the same for them.

It was still a wonder to her, though.

Reaching out, she dared to skim her fingers ever so lightly over Caleb's face. She loved touching him, exploring him, and couldn't wait to do the same with Jesse and Justin. For now though, there was only Caleb, the feel of his strong features beneath her fingertips. She couldn't get enough of touching him, them. She danced her fingers over him, trying not to wake him. Just the slightest caress of his cheekbone, brushing her fingers across his mouth, especially that slightly fuller upper lip, then along his jaw. The softest butterfly trace down his throat, over the firm muscles of his chest, the ripples of his abs. She was fascinated with exploring him. His cock was already a little firm. She slid her fingertips over it ever so lightly.

"I'll give you an hour to stop doing that," he murmured. "Or more."

She looked up to see his half-open sleepy eyes darken, watching her as she touched him.

It was amazing to Caleb to come awake to that ephemeral touch, to open his eyes to see her rapt expression and the slight curve of her lips. To see her pleasure at touching him.

She tightened ever so slightly as Justin moved against her. His hardening cock pressed against her hip.

"You can't say I didn't warn you," he said.

Jesse kissed her belly, sucked at the spot just above the inside of her hip that made her tighten, then slid up her body to impale her on his shaft as he took her mouth.

She sighed with pleasure as he filled her. It was sheer heaven to find herself so full of him. He rocked his hips smoothly, driving his cock into her in a delightfully slow, incredibly tantalizing, rhythm.

Looking at his brothers, he said, "Beat you."

She struggled not to laugh at his smug look, not wanting to lose the feel of him inside her.

He looked down at her. "God, you're so tight, and you feel so good."

She rolled her hips in return, wrapping her legs around his to take him deeper.

Jesse groaned, shifting to feel her tightness around his shaft, and she quivered. Her eyelids fluttered as he thrust more deeply, more steadily.

Her hand was still curled around Caleb's cock as he watched his brother fuck her, and he shared it as Ceili's fingers tightened around him, worked him in time to Jesse's deep steady thrusts.

Justin groaned as her fingers curled around his shaft.

Ceili's eyes closed as she took Jesse deeper into her, her hips pumping.

She closed more tightly around him.

"God, that's good," he said as pleasure pulsed within his cock.

Feeling Jesse swelling inside her, Ceili tightened around him, her hips lifting to take him more deeply still.

Jesse came on a long low moan of sheer pleasure.

All unnoticed by Ceili, rapt as she was with touching him as Jesse took his pleasure, Justin had shifted, giving Caleb a look. He slipped out her grasp as Jesse collapsed beside her.

Caleb drew Ceili back against him, his cock sliding inside her as Jesse suckled at her breast.

She drew in a long breath as she felt Caleb's rigid shaft fill her, letting her head fall back against his shoulder at the pleasure of feeling his pulsing cock inside her.

Caleb knew the moment Justin's mouth found her clit, as that breath she took caught and her eyelashes fluttered against his cheek. Her body tightened around his shaft.

It had been sheer delight to feel Caleb's long hard cock fill her, but an even greater one to feel him so deep inside her as Justin's thumbs exposed her clit. His mouth closed on her and he sucked slowly and steadily on that tender bud as he flicked it with his tongue, and she jolted as a shot of pleasure raced through her.

She tightened around Caleb's pulsing length, as his arm held her in place for both him and Justin.

Each movement of Justin's mouth caused her to close and tighten around Caleb's cock. It was like being stroked by her body.

Jesse nipped at her nipple while Caleb toyed, tugged and tormented the other.

Both nipples were aching, as hard as pebbles.

Justin's mouth drove her up higher, teasing her clit with little flicks of his tongue, while Caleb's hips pumped hard and steady to drive his swelling cock deeper inside her.

Ceili's internal muscles almost seemed to ripple around Caleb's shaft, tightening in response to Justin's mouth on her clit and Caleb fucked her slowly and steadily. She was trembling, quivering, her body tightening around him.

"Please," she whispered, her hands clenched in the bedclothes, her hips moving, shifting, searching for completion. She tightened around him. "Oh, please."

Caleb drove hard and deep inside her as Justin suckled at her clit.

She came with a cry, her back arching as she tightened, her internal muscles pulsing as her orgasm took her. And him with her.

With a deep groan, Ceili heard Caleb's ecstasy, as he came only seconds behind her, his body locked against her as his hips thrust, driving him deeper as his pleasure pumped into her.

It was incredible.

He wrapped his arms around her. All she could do was smile.

"Now that's the way to wake up. Good morning, Ceili," Jesse said, grinning.

"Good morning to all of you, too," Ceili said, shaking her head, dazed and limp.

"As much as I hate to say it," Caleb said, reluctantly, brushing his lips over the curve of her ear, "but it is time to get up."

Curling in tighter against Ceili, Jesse murmured, "I was already up."

With a grin, Ceili rolled her eyes, looking at Caleb. He smiled back and shook his head at his brother

"You're were off yesterday, you're on today," Caleb reminded him.

Jesse groaned as Justin reached for Ceili's crutches.

"Will you be all right alone here for the rest of the day?" Caleb asked her as they made use of what seemed to be the communal bathroom. All their shaving gear was laid out there.

Justin found a spare toothbrush for her.

"If nothing else, Ranger will keep me busy," she said, "but as long as I can borrow a computer, I'll be fine, as long as you don't mind me being here invading your space. I work from home, but my computer got fried in the fire. Now, at least, I might be able to arrange for an advance on my pay so I can buy some clothes to replace what was burned."

"Mind, she says," Justin muttered. "As if we'd mind that she let us fuck her to our hearts content."

Ceili laughed. "You'll get tired of me soon enough."

Wrapping an arm around her, Justin looked down at her. "Not likely."

The look in his eyes caught at her.

"You can use my computer," Jesse said. "I'll set you up with your own login."

"Jesse's our resident geek," Caleb explained. "As for clothes, take one of my tee shirts for now."

"Given how tall you are, it's more likely to be a dress for me. I'll let you guys shower and shave, since you have priority," Ceili said. "Meet you downstairs."

It was Ranger's barks and the smells from the kitchen that drew them – coffee, eggs frying, bread toasting.

Walking into the kitchen they found Ceili dancing, almost literally, balanced on her crutches, completely oblivious to their arrival as she waited for the bread finish toasting. Irish step dancing, Riverdance style, to music only she could hear. All she wore was one of Caleb's tee shirts. Her hair glowed, her breasts swayed as her good foot moved in the intricate steps, her hips shifting in quick-time now and then. She was graceful, fluid, even with the crutches. Ranger danced around her, going from one side of her to the other. It was easy to tell this was a morning ritual for them.

Leaning against a doorjamb, Justin said, with a smile. "Now we know why you were named Ceili."

Startled, she spun on one crutch, nearly overbalanced, and blushed before grinning wryly. "My mother used to say I was dancing before I was born, and that's how I got the name."

The toast popped up. She waved at the center island where they usually just grabbed something quick and easy to eat. "Sit."

Ranger obeyed first, as usual.

Laughing, she tossed him a piece of toast before dishing up full plates.

They followed the dog's example as she slid the plates to them.

It was a real breakfast. Omelets, toast, coffee.

Caleb took a bite. Savored it. It was wonderful. "What's in that?"

She laughed. "It would be better if I had fresh mushrooms and spinach rather than canned, but I worked with what I had. And you did have onions and feta cheese."

"Real food," Jesse said, chowing down, and looked at Caleb. "Can we keep her, Caleb, can we, can we?"

Caleb laughed and gave Ceili a look. "I'm certainly willing to give it a try."

As much as it warmed Ceili to hear him, them, say it, it also brought reality crashing down on her. Although it made her heart ache, this could only be temporary. "Don't get too used to me," she said, softly. "I can't stay in one place too long, I won't risk making any of you targets."

Hearing what Caleb did in her voice, the banked longing, the need, loneliness, and regret, he looked at Jesse and Justin. They put it together, too. So much made sense now.

Caleb looked at Ceili, at the expression in her eyes before she averted them to fetch more toast.

All her neighbors had spoken well of her, even though she'd only been in the apartment a few months. She been willing to help anyone who asked. Almost universally they spoke of her being kind and funny.

She was also pretty, shapely, but none of them had mentioned a significant other of any kind. Or even a date. He'd wondered about that. With that hair, those blue eyes, and those curves, there should have been at least one.

But he had the impression she hadn't dared to let anyone get too close. It was a lonely way to live, and, as they had seen, that wasn't her nature.

It was he and his brothers who had gotten past her barriers.

"Who got hurt?" he asked, remembering her concern over the wounded officer. It was a leap, but one he was used to making. He had to make quick judgments all the time.

She went still for a moment, took a breath, and then looked at him. "No one, yet, at least not badly, although it was a near thing. Thank heavens. The man who trained Ranger, Tom. He was an ex-cop. Ex-military. With canine units." She sighed, her mouth tightening. "I thought it was safe. I'd been careful, I thought, not to leave a paper trail."

She closed her eyes for a moment. "I don't think, though, he really understood how bad it was. He was dropping me off at my apartment. Somehow, he knew or sensed something wrong, something was off. He was trying to protect me. It was close. Like yesterday. Bullets flying everywhere, anyone could have been hurt. Someone at the motel. Or like the officer who was shot." Caleb saw the sick fear in her eyes as she looked at him. Not of him, for him. "Or one of your people. Even with your body armor, all it would take would be a chance shot or a ricochet. Then there's you, Jesse, Justin. Each of you different, but you've been so kind to me, and you're each so wonderful. I wanted to keep my distance, but something about each one of you got past that. You're all First Responders, I know, you take chances every day, but not like this. If anything happened to Jesse or Justin, or to any of your team, Caleb, you'd hate me for putting them in danger and I wouldn't blame you." Tom's wife had. "If any of you gets hurt because of me… I can't face that. I just can't."

She closed her eyes, her hand on her stomach.

The woman had courage, Caleb had to give her that, and he knew his brothers saw that in her, too. She was on the run. Alone. With no one to protect her except her dog. No family, or at least none close. Both parents were dead, which explained her self-sufficiency. And if any were, they'd be targets, too, hostages.

"It didn't happen, Ceili," he said, going around the island to put his arms around her. She looked up at him. "And it won't. We're prepared now. Everyone on my team recognized those men as ex-military. Jesse and Justin know now, too." He looked at her, his gaze on hers. "And I wouldn't hate you, Ceili, but I'd would those responsible. And that's not you. You didn't ask for this."

Now Jesse understood. He'd known she was as attracted to him he was to her, and keeping a distance wasn't her nature, although she'd tried, until he'd surprised them both by giving in to his when he'd kissed her. Now he knew why she hadn't called. It wasn't because he'd mistaken her attraction to him, he hadn't been wrong there, but that she knew staying would put him at risk if they came after her again.

"I served a couple of tours in Iraq and Afghanistan, Ceili," he said. "Justin did, too. We both went through Ranger training."

With a nod, Justin said, "As a medic, but even medics come under fire. I had the same training Jesse did. I have a question, though, Ceili? Why didn't they put you in witness protection?"

"With the trial over, I wasn't a witness anymore," Ceili answered, with a sigh. "With Janssen out of the country, although there are international warrants out on him, he's in a country with no joint extradition treaty. The case was closed. He wasn't our problem anymore, so they had no on-going reason to do so. And he hasn't been linked to the attacks on me, any more than he has any of the others who displeased him. He sends his mercenaries to do the dirty work. Only now he's being more careful. The first time he'd hired street thugs, addicts who'd have done anything for a fix. I can't prove that, but I suspect I'm right. Everyone, including the cops, chalked it up to a woman walking alone at night. The break-in of my apartment could have been thieves, home invaders. It's common enough. I was just lucky I'm pretty flexible and I can fit in tight spaces, although a few bits got squashed. I heard them talking, their frustration, but they weren't giving up. Nothing links those attacks to a specific source. There is no clear, compelling reason to spend hundreds of thousands of dollars to protect someone against the boogey man."

"There's got to be a way," Justin said, "to make it stop."

He looked at Caleb.

Caleb nodded. "We just have to find it."

He looked to Ceili.

"Maybe it's time to put your research skills to work for yourself," he said. "Can you get me all the data on the findings and testimony at the grand jury and the trials? All your reports. We'll go over them, maybe fresh eyes will see something no one else did. All we can do is try."

He had a few other ideas, too, but that came first.

"Jesse, take Ceili down to your computer cave, get her set up. Ceili, send everything to me at my department e-mail," Caleb said.

With a nod, Jesse swept her up to toss her over his shoulder.

"Jesse!" she exclaimed as he started toward the stairs. She looked at his brothers. "Why does he keep doing this?" She narrowed her eyes at them. "And why are you laughing?"

"I'm doing it because a. –I can and I enjoy it, b. – you have a very fine ass, and c. – the crutches slow you down," Jesse answered.

"What he said," Justin added.

Caleb said, "And she does have a very fine ass."

"I can hear you," she said.

It was impossible not to laugh.

They disappeared, Ranger at Jesse's heels.

Justin looked at Caleb. "You've got a plan."

Taking a breath, considering it, Caleb said, "The beginning of a plan. If they give us the time and chance. I'm not ready to share it with Ceili and get her hopes up, but maybe we can turn the tables. Turn the hunters into the hunted. Once we have more information, we can also call in a few favors of our own. Find out who's gone rogue or become a mercenary. I'll also talk to Jeff to let him know what we might be dealing with."

*****

When Caleb had described Jesse's sanctuary as a computer cave, he hadn't been kidding. It was dominated by a monster of a TV, linked to a surround sound system, a computer, and gaming chairs. He settled her in one of the chairs.

On one side was a display of Manga, posters and comics, on another was graphic novels, and at the back a D & D setup.

Bemused, she looked at Jesse. "Wow. My big tough firefighter is also a serious geek."

He grinned as he fired up his system. "Only a few of the guys at the station know about my 'hobby', so don't give me away."

"I wouldn't dream of it," she said in amazement. "I'm impressed."

"I have my own server down here," he said, as the TV screen blossomed to life. Her name appeared under an icon. "Give yourself a password and you're good to go. Here's Caleb's police department e-mail. Give me your phone, I'll put our numbers in and get it charged."

She nodded, distracted, fingers flying over the keyboard.

Watching her, Jesse grinned, "A girl after my own heart."

Looking up into his blue-gray eyes, at the warmth in them, she had to smile.

"I might surprise you. Tell Caleb I sent him the link and password to the files he wanted."

Jesse saw a shadow move in her eyes as she briefly sobered. "I saved a lot of my research up to the cloud. After the break-in I saved everything I'd found to another location, in case I needed it. I'm glad I did, although I never anticipated this. Before I did, reporter wanted to do a story on Janssen, her research led her to me. We did the interview and

I gave her access to what I'd found. She died shortly after she published. A car accident, they said. A lot of the people Janssen doesn't like die that way. Accidents, or made to look like accidents. As they tried. But Caleb might want to read her expose series first."

Brushing her hair back, Jesse kissed her softly. "Just so you know, you're safe for the moment, and we intend to keep you that way."

"Why?" she asked softly. Because she needed to know. Had to.

"Because we like you, you're smart, funny and a little nuts. You fit right in. And you don't deserve this," he answered. "And because I, personally, like you a lot. We'll figure it out. We've been through the wars, both real and personal. All of us had to learn to think on our feet, and on the job we did and the ones we do. Trust us."

Something in her eased. She grinned. "In case you hadn't noticed, I already do."

"I had, as a matter of fact."

This time, he took her mouth with intent, crushing it beneath his as her fingers slid into his hair to pull his mouth harder against hers. He kissed her thoroughly, hungrily. And she did the same.

"You'd better go," she said, her voice husky. "I can't get enough of you, any of you."

She let out a long sigh, smiling dreamily.

"I'll get your crutches. If you need anything, text us."

# Chapter Eight

As Caleb walked to the garage, he texted Jeff Parker, the lead for their SWAT division, asking for an all-hands-on deck meeting regarding the situation the previous night. Jeff was a good man, experienced, and, like many on the force and in SWAT, ex-military. In his case a Marine.

First, though, Caleb wanted to take a look through the information Ceili had sent him.

After changing into his uniform – many cities had found it was expensive to keep highly trained personnel like himself strictly as SWAT – so he filled other roles on crime details, serving high risk warrants, crowd control, protection details – but until the meeting he had a little time free. So, he accessed the info she'd sent, scanned the article and the details of the trial.

What he read wasn't reassuring, especially where Ceili was concerned. In fact, it chilled him. Janssen's mercenaries served a lot of functions, including as his personal hit squad. The number of deaths, cumulatively, was disturbing, if unnoticed by most due to having taken place in different countries.

One thing she hadn't sent, and he realized it was like her to do it, were the attacks on her personally. So, he ran her name for more than just wants and warrants. He winced mentally when he saw the report on the first attack. It wasn't just her nose they'd broken, or the split in her eyebrow. The break-in at her apartment was on record. The men who'd done it had fled when they'd heard the approaching sirens, as the neighbors and Ceili herself had reported – after the responding officers had moved the refrigerator behind which she'd wedged herself. The attempted hit and run wasn't on record, but the attack involving her dog trainer was. Cuts and scratches from exploding glass, and a ricochet off a car window pillar that had creased the man's arm. From then on, there had been incidents in different cities.

Everyone was filing in as he arrived, Jeff was already there and waiting.

"You want to fill me in first, or once and done."

"Once and done, and you're not going to like it."

Jeff's eyes narrowed. Caleb handed him the printouts. As Jeff read, his expression grew grim.

Scanning the room, Caleb could see everyone who should be was there. He looked at Jeff, who glanced over the group and nodded.

"Okay, heads-up people," Jeff said. "Caleb…"

"Some of you may have heard what happened last night but some of you may not," Caleb said,
"So here it is in a nutshell. My team was called out on a report of automatic weapons fire at a motel. We responded to find one shooter firing from the cover of parked cars at the front of the building – probably to keep the guests heads down and in their rooms on the off chance someone was armed. We all know that was about as unlikely as one of those carrying to shoot back. The third shooter was the first sign this wasn't a drug or gang thing, or a domestic."

"Two others were up on the second level trying to enter a room. When two of my team moved in to take out the covering shooter, he opened fire on us, and retreated using standard military tactics, strafing our positions to keep us pinned down until their target was acquired. He was covering the stairs for their escape. The shooters at the top, though, found they had a surprise waiting – the victim, Ceili Whelan, and her attack-trained dog."

"Ranger's a pussycat once he knows you," one of Caleb's team said. "Great dog."

Caleb couldn't disagree, even with the slipper incident. He preferred bare feet anyway.

"The shooters were wearing full body armor and worked as a military unit. So, they were prepared for police intervention and possibly even SWAT. They weren't prepared for her, or for her to fight back."

"Here's what we know about the intended victim," Caleb said, trying to keep it clinical, impersonal, even as the memory of her in that thin tee shirt whispered through his mind. And the way she'd responded to his kiss, his touch, her body rising to meet his. With an effort, he put it aside. "Name, Ceili Whelan. Two, almost three, years ago she was a researcher involved in a high-profile court case. Her research and testimony helped bring down a foreign-born, naturalized American drug kingpin by the name of Lukas Janssen who started out in pharmaceuticals, then expanded his 'business' into the illegal side, running it by computer, with ex-military and mercenaries as his enforcers and assassins. When law enforcement here moved in, he successfully fled the country. First by way of Canada, then to a country that has, so far, refused to extradite him. He's continued his business from overseas, although it was severely crippled here."

"Where's the victim now?" Gordon asked.

"After this latest attack, and there have been several priors, she sustained a mild concussion and a sprained ankle. I have her stashed in a safe house while she recovers."

One of his people, Jax, said, "So she's been doing what for more than two years?"

Caleb took a breath. "Running, trying, not always successfully, to stay one step ahead of them."

"For over two years?" Jax said, appalled. "How, for Christ's sake?"

"She's smart, resilient, and tougher than she looks," Caleb answered, trying to keep his feelings about Ceili to himself. She was all of that. Just the thought of her reminded him of the night before, that thin t-shirt, and the warmth in her eyes when she'd looked up to see him. And he loved her fascination, her sheer pleasure in touching him, and more than just touching. Making love to her, her marvelous responsiveness. He also remembered her 'dancing' with Ranger that morning and had to restrain a smile. The question, though, also triggered a spark of anger. "She works from home, still in research. In the past, when attacked, she fled to another city. Let's make sure she doesn't have to run anymore."

Whatever happened between the four of them, Ceili, his brothers and himself, he wanted to give her that. Serve and protect, that's what he did. If he couldn't do it for sweet mercurial Ceili then what was the point? She'd shown him more affection and been more responsive in two days than Alison ever had.

"So how do we do that?" someone else asked. "What can we do?

"Find them," Jeff said, his tone unequivocal. "By all accounts this woman did her job to help shut down a major drug pipeline in this country. She shouldn't have to pay for it. So, let's do our job. These men made their choice, now they have to pay for it. Those of you who have confidential informants tap them, tell them what we're looking for. We need names and descriptions. Those of you with military backgrounds, tap those sources. Find out who's gone rogue or taken the mercenary route and might not be too picky about who hires them, who they work for. No one gets away with shooting up our city. We're cops, that's what we do, protect the citizens of this city. She's now one of ours."

Caleb couldn't have asked for more. His people were some of the best he'd ever worked with, and he'd have fought beside any of them any day and did.

"Keep your eyes open everyone," Caleb said. "Anything that smacks remotely of these guys, call for backup."

"Dismissed," Jeff said, before turning to Caleb. "Wherever you've got the lady stashed, keep her there and keep it on the q.t."

"I intend to," Caleb said, although thoughts of explaining where Ceili was would be…difficult.

"In the meantime, I'm going to reach out to the prosecutor who handled that case and learn as much as I can."

"And I've got a warrant to serve," Caleb said.

*****

Caleb had said to put her research skills to work for her own benefit, but she had her job first, the one that paid the bills. After Ceili contacted the research company and told them about the fire, they agreed to give her a small advance. They'd also given her work to do to earn it. She'd also have to go to the bank to get her new charge cards, but they hadn't been delivered yet. If she needed to run… Just the thought of having to leave Jesse, Justin, and Caleb nearly broke her heart, but if she had to, to keep them safe, she would.

She found some hamburger in the freezer, set some out to defrost, cooked some of it up for Ranger, adding some frozen vegetables, and some oatmeal she found in a cabinet.

In between doing the job she was paid to do, which today meant comparisons of actuarial tables, she set up a search for Lukas Janssen, filtering out those without his pharmaceutical and computer backgrounds, with a Dutch and US passport. She also set up a simultaneous search for anyone associated with Janssen's trial, as well as the doctors, pharmacists, and others who'd been convicted, or had turned state's evidence.

While that was running, she did her comparisons, found the information requested, and wrote up her findings. All in all, that last was pretty boring stuff.

To ease the tedium, she also did a little research on a more… personal…level. As she explored, a little trickle of excitement went through her. She grinned. This would be fun.

When Ranger got restless, she took him outside, and found a frisbee in the common area. Throwing it and getting him to bring it back were two different things, though, as usual. He wanted to play tug or keep away. Tug she could do. Keep away, though, was hard on crutches. When she did successfully get it away from him, he chased it with delight.

She was still working though, so she called him back. He brought the frisbee, too, and she knew she'd have to distract him to get it away from him. In the meantime, he chewed on it.

On her return she found the results of her searches. Looking at them, for a moment she could only sit there trying to absorb it.

Whatever the trial in the states had accomplished, Janssen was still very much involved in the illegal drug trade, heroin, cocaine, meth, and fentanyl. Although most of his activities were overseas, she could see signs he was trying to get back into the American market. And with him, his own personal cadre of mercenaries – ex-military, some of whom had been involved in some shady activities in Afghanistan and Iraq. They'd carried over the torture techniques from there, like water-boarding, as well as inventing a few of their own. Cross him and he'd unleash them on the source of his displeasure. However long it took. More than once, examples had been made.

She had the list of those involved in the trial, both the good guys and the bad, and started to work on that, searching for their current status. The bad guys, anyone who'd been

mentioned during the trial, she sorted out into a document and
sent it to Caleb.

It was getting late, she wasn't certain what time they
would all be home, but she remembered how much they'd
enjoyed breakfast.

Well, she was a researcher, she thought with a grin, and
searched to find the standard schedule for firefighters and
police officers here. She knew most worked shift work, and in
some cities or counties firefighters, EMTs and paramedics
could be on 10-12-hour shifts, while in others they worked
twenty-four hours in a row – bunking at the firehouse. Since
Justin and Jesse had both been home the previous night, and
Caleb had mentioned that Jesse was off the next day, she
guessed they were on 10- or 12-hour shifts. Although they
could still work twenty-fours.

She did the math and then went with Ranger up the stairs
to search the kitchen. A check of the trash can had shown a
lot of takeout, typical for three men living together. Meals
came out of boxes of one kind or another. The exception was
a box of decent spaghetti, but no sauce. With a little of the
milk for cereal added to the shredded mozzarella and
parmesan cheeses she'd found when she'd made breakfast,
she'd have something like a white sauce. At the back of the
freezer she found a bag of frozen peeled shrimp. She also
found a jar of garlic. She sautéed the garlic and shrimp,
letting the shrimp defrost in the pan, then set the heat on low
to cook off the water. A few shakes from a jar of Italian
spices went into the sauté, while Ranger finished off the
hamburger. Everything went over the spaghetti in a large pan,
including some of the defrosted vegetables, for a kind of
pasta primavera with shrimp. A quick taste assured her it was
edible.

Then she hobbled up to the shower, turning the tap to get
the water hot.

With a smile she remembered the workout she'd gotten both that morning and the evening before as she stepped into the hot water, she had some stiff muscles here and there, so she washed her hair then let the water run over her.

To her surprise soap-lathered hands slid over and around her breasts and belly in a slippery caress as lips brushed over her ear. His fingers tried to capture her soapy nipples. Her breath caught.

"Need a hand?"

She knew that voice and turned in his arms to look up into his handsome face and golden eyes.

"Justin," she said, delighted.

"Jesse and Caleb should be along shortly, but I couldn't resist. And since you're still on crutches, I thought you might need a little assistance."

One of his hands slid over the curve of her ass, down into the cleavage between them, the other slid between her thighs.

Justin watched her face as he played, teasing her. Her eyes never left his as her hands went to his shoulders for balance, and then tightened as her lips parted. Her breasts rose and fell as he stroked her clit, pressed a finger against the tight rosette of her ass. Water rinsed the soap from his fingers, and he slid one inside her pussy to her gasp. She was damp, and not just from the water.

"That's my girl," he said, as he found her clit, stroking as she trembled.

He pressed a finger a little harder against her darker channel as he flicked her clit, and her eyes widened as he breached that tight sphincter slowly and gently. He stroked her delicate bud as he pushed his finger deeper into her. He slid a finger into her pussy, then back out again to pinch and play with her clit.

"Let me watch you come," he said, as he drove her higher.

And she did, coming with a cry as she shook and quivered, her eyes widening but never leaving his.

He took her sweet mouth, sliding his fingers out of her to pull her hips against him. Steadying her out of the shower, he sat on the bench beneath the window with her in his lap to dry her off.

Ceili loved it. Reaching up to stroke her fingers over his cheekbone, more defined than either Caleb's or Jesse's, over the strong line of his jaw, she was entirely aware of his cock twitching beneath her. She kissed his firm mouth, then trailed her lips down the lean hard muscles of his chest, explored the taut muscles of his abs, bracing herself on his thighs as she slid slowly to the floor. Looking up at him, she smiled. Now she could practice what she'd learned earlier.

The feel of her mouth and tongue on him made Justin's abs tighten. He leaned back against the wall, closing his eyes in pleasure as her lips explored him, wandering over his abs, his thighs. It was delightfully maddening. Then her tongue swirled around the head of his cock, exploring it, exploring him. It flicked across the slit and his abs tightened in response to the heated rush that shot through him. He grasped the edges of the bench to keep from plunging his hands into her hair.

Then her lips slid over him, to take him into her mouth.

She took him deep, finding out how much of him she could take, and he thought he'd lose his mind as she filled her mouth with him. He stroked her hair back, trying to control himself enough to let her set her rhythm. Then she ran her fingers lightly around his balls, and all his attention was on what she was doing to him. His hands tightened in her hair.

Ceili basked in the taste of Justin, of his skin, of the little bit of pre-cum at the back of her throat, and hummed with pleasure, almost purred with it as he swelled and throbbed in her mouth. He groaned, and she sucked on him in earnest, sliding her mouth up and down his shaft, pausing to glide her tongue around the broad head of his cock, finding the small indentation there. He jolted. Delighted, she slid her tongue across the slit at the top, and his hands locked in her hair. She drove her mouth down over as much of him as she could take, her throat working. His cock was rigid, throbbing as she sucked on him steadily.

She was driving Justin insane, all control nearly gone.

With an effort, he held her head still.

"If you don't stop that, I'm going to come," he warned, and dear God, he wanted to.

As if that was what she had been waiting for, she took a deep breath and took him as deep as she could. He could feel her throat working as she drew back and then sucked him back.

Control vanished as a rush of pure pleasure shot through him. His body arched as he came, thrusting, the ecstasy of it overwhelming. Her hands locked on his hips as the first gush of his cum filled her throat. He jolted in delight as she swallowed, then she pulled back, her hand closing around him to stroke, drawing out his pleasure. His warm cum spurted over her lovely, lush breasts.

She looked at him and licked her lips almost curiously.

"Damn, Ceili," he said. His mind didn't seem to want to work.

"So," she said, looking up at him in delight. "I did good?"

"You did damn good," he said.

"Not all the research I did today was for work," she said, pertly, grinning.

He shook his head at her. "You amaze me."

"I did warn you I'm curious. About a lot of things. If you're going to do something, you should do it right. It seemed only fair. That mouth of yours has done as much for me."

"You are something, Ceili."

Her eyes and expression went soft. "So are you, Justin."

She looked at her cum-covered breasts. "But now I'm going to have to wash up again."

Both heard the door close downstairs and Ranger raced out to see who it was.

"And I'm going to have to get dressed," he said. "That is, if I can stand."

He pulled her up into his arms, then gave her a hand into the shower to kiss her sweet and hard. Shaking his head in wonder, he held her hair back.

Ceili washed the evidence of his pleasure off with a little regret, she couldn't mind the scent of him on her skin.

He gave her another quick kiss before he disappeared down the hall.

Then she tugged her tee shirt on and made her way down the stairs.

"Whatever that is," Caleb said, gathering her into his arms for a kiss, "it smells incredible."

"It's pasta primavera with shrimp. Sort of. Hungry?"

His stomach growled. "Starving."

She grinned at the sound, "So I hear. So how did your day go?"

"Other than the usual, I had to serve an arrest warrant on a member of a biker gang," he answered as she turned on the toaster oven, then stirred the primavera before dishing up a good portion onto a plate. She handed it to him as the toaster oven dinged. She opened it and the smell of garlic toast wafted out into the room. She slid it onto a dish and put it in the center of the island as she dished up another plate.

"Why do I think they probably didn't take that well?" she asked.

"Well, they're not big on law enforcement to start, and being arrested even less so," he said. "Things got a little, um, heated."

She eyed him.

"Guns drawn on both sides. I had to do some fast talking to keep it from escalating, but it helped to have backup already outside waiting. But we had a few tense moments there."

Justin came in to join them and she handed him the plate she'd dished up for him, taking a smaller one for herself.

"I saw your car in the garage and wondered where you were," Caleb said. "How did your day go?"

"About the usual," Justin said. "A possible heart attack, someone crashed one of those silly scooters, and a fender bender where one driver complained of whiplash. Served him right, it would have been less likely if his eyes had been on the road and not on his phone."

"How did work go, Ceili?" Caleb asked.

She crossed her eyes. "I may be curious, but actuaries are boring. Actuary tables even more so. I thought I'd lose my mind. Do you have any balls around that you don't mind being chewed on?"

"Ranger?" he asked.

"He needs something to chase. He found someone's frisbee when I took him out the other day and brought it back here, but I don't know where he hid it."

"Hang on," Justin said, and disappeared, returning juggling three balls, catching Ranger's complete attention.

The dog barked happily, jumping to his feet, and then around Justin, leaping into the air to try to catch one.

"I'll take him out, let him run around," Justin said.

"That would be wonderful, Justin. Just keep in mind that he doesn't fetch. He likes to chase balls, then it becomes a game of keep-away, tug, and wrestle."

Justin grinned. "We'll get along just fine. I always wanted a dog, but with our schedules? Come on, Ranger, want to go play?"

Barking and leaping around him for the ball, Ranger followed Justin out.

"Just to let you know," Caleb said, with a laugh. "Ranger found the other slipper."

Ceili winced.

"Hey, at least it wasn't a shoe, and I prefer to go barefoot around the house anyway. Which reminds me, I want to change into something more comfortable."

He gave her a kiss and went up the stairs.

Ceili picked up the plates, and started to fill the dishwasher, but the memory of Caleb without his shirt haunted her. She turned and followed him, using the railing, not the crutch.

As she entered the bedroom, her breath caught.

The words escaped her before she could stop herself. "Oh, my," she said softly.

Caleb turned to find Ceili looking at him, her expression soft, her pretty lips parted, those blue eyes on his.

"Please," she whispered, as she stepped toward him.

He caught her hands to steady her as she lifted her head to look at him.

All he wanted was her mouth, to take it, to ravage it, so he did, and she ravaged his in return as her hands slid up his arms to his shoulders, wrapping around his neck.

He backed them to the bed, caught the hem of her tee shirt, pulled it over head and tossed it away as he drew her on to the bed.

"No," she said, brushing her lips over his, then his jaw, down his throat, "let me. I've been dreaming of this since I saw you the first time without a shirt."

Her mouth, tongue and hands explored him, caressed and stroked. He lost himself in her touch.

Ceili loved the feel and taste of him, trailing her lips over his collarbone, brushing them over the smooth strong curve of the muscles of his chest, the firm ripples of his abs. He was so beautiful, every muscle defined, his belly flat and taut. She dipped her tongue into his navel, kissed, licked and nibbled just above and along his hips, feeling him tighten as she pushed his sweatpants off his hips and his shaft sprang free.

Heat poured low in Caleb's belly as Ceili's mouth left a trail of fire over him, making his cock throb and ache as his balls tightened. Then her warm wet mouth slid over his rigid member, taking it deep. He could feel the muscles in the back of her throat work to take him, and his body locked with the sheer pleasure of it. Then she began to suck on him, her mouth sliding up so her tongue could swirl around the head. Just when he thought he couldn't get any harder, go any higher, her tongue slid over the sensitive notch in the head, swirled around it to lick the small spurt of pre-cum from it. His hands locked in her hair as his hips pumped, he couldn't stop himself. And she hummed with pleasure, the sound and vibration driving him up another notch. She took a long breath and then met his next thrust, taking him deep.

Caleb exploded, filling her mouth. Her hands locked around his hips as she sucked him, her throat working to take him, to swallow some of what he gave her before pulling back, her hand stroking him as he emptied himself over her.

He looked up at her, at her pleasure in giving him his.

She smiled radiantly.

"That was amazing," she said, her voice a little unsteady, before collapsing limply beside him.

"You're amazing," he said. "Are you all right? Some women don't like doing that."

She frowned a little. "Why? You do it for me. It seems only fair. And I wanted to try it." She grinned, looking a little abashed. "But I'm still practicing. You said I should use some of my research skills for myself. So, I did. You can blame Justin, he's the one who piqued my curiosity. Otherwise, I'm fine, although I'm more than a little hot and bothered, but I'm pretty sure one of you will help me out there. Not right this minute, but eventually."

"Jess isn't back yet, but none of us can seem to get enough of you," Caleb said. "I'll be right back."

He was, armed with a warm wet washcloth and proceeded to clean them both up then tossed the washcloth into his laundry basket.

They moved up the bed and he wrapped an arm around her shoulders to pull her close.

Ceili slid one of hers across his abdomen, caressing him as she did. "I don't think I'll ever get tired of touching you."

Stroking her breast, toying with the nipple, he said. "I have the same problem."

Glancing at the clock, he said, "Jesse's running late, either he's making up some hours, or they had a fire."

Ranger came bounding in, followed by Justin and Ceili held up a hand to the dog, narrowing her eyes at him. "Don't even think about it. No dogs on the bed. There have to be some limits."

Justin was already drawing his tee shirt over his head and tossing it at the laundry basket.

The dog's eyes lit up. He darted toward the laundry basket, snatched up the tee shirt. Justin kicked the door shut as Ranger tried to bolt past him.

"Ranger," Ceili said firmly. "No. Put it down. We don't eat clothes. You know that."

Caleb had shifted to watch, smothering laughter.

The dog plopped his butt down, looked at Justin, affronted, then sighed and dropped the shirt.

"Good dog. Now, lay down. Go ahead, Justin, toss it again."

Justin picked up the shirt and tossed it in the laundry basket.

The dog started to move, and Ceili said, "Ranger," warningly. The dog subsided, dropping his head to his paws with a sigh. "Life with dog," Ceili said, trying not to laugh, shaking her head while Justin stripped off the rest of his clothes before opening the door again.

He ruffled the dog's ears as he joined Ceili and Caleb, with Caleb curled up beside her, his hand across her waist. She ran a hand down his arm to clasp his wrist.

Justin gave her a quick kiss, laying his head on her shoulder, lightly caressing one of her breasts. "That dog is too smart by half."

"You have no idea."

They tried to watch some movie, but it wasn't nearly as good as some had implied.

Both men were asleep within minutes. So was she.

The sound of the downstairs door opening and closing woke Ceili.

A few moments later she heard Jesse on the stairs. He peered into the room.

Her voice soft, Ceili said, "Where have you been?"

Both Caleb and Justin had shifted a little while they slept. Pulling his tee shirt off wearily, unbuckling his belt, Jesse shoved his pants off as well, then slid up her body to wrap his arms around her hips, kissing her belly before laying his head on it with a sigh.

She could smell smoke as she stroked his hair. "A fire?"

"Warehouse," he murmured.

"Go to sleep, love," she said. "Tell me about it in the morning."

His arms tightened around her hips as he nuzzled her belly. "Better than a pillow."

She smiled, stroking his hair until his breathing evened out.

# Chapter Nine

Caleb's alarm went off softly. Reaching quickly but carefully, he shut it off, then looked at his brothers. Jesse's head rested on the softest part of Ceili's firm belly, his arms curled around her hips as if she were a pillow. Ceili's blue eyes were open.

She smiled warmly, sleepily. "Morning, love."

"Good morning, yourself," he said, the endearment catching at him. He lowered his mouth to her soft one for a long lingering kiss and felt her sigh of pleasure as she met it, her lips parting for him. She lifted her arm to run her fingers into his hair

"When did Jesse get home?" he asked, quietly.

"I don't know the time, but it was late," she answered, softly. "A warehouse fire."

He caressed her breast, toyed lightly with the nipple. Her head went back as her eyelids fluttered, a soft sound escaping her. Yet she kept the rest of her body still so as not to wake his brothers. He liked the idea of her trapped by them while he took his pleasure of her. Lowering his head, his hand cupping her breast, he drew the crest of it in to suckle it in hard steady pulls. He felt her twitch, soft sounds escaping her.

Ceili thought she'd lose her mind as Caleb suckled at one breast, and then Justin's hand closed around the other, and he drew the tip into his mouth to suck sleepily at it.

Propping his head on his hand, Caleb toyed with her nipple as he watched Justin suck the other, while Jesse slept, unaware.

Every muscle in Ceili's upper body was taut. He lowered his mouth to her breast again, sucked hard. She moaned softly.

"I think we could make you come just by sucking on
your breasts," he said.

Her blue eyes looked at him and Justin beseechingly. Her
hand searched for and found the head of his now-rigid cock
and closed around it. He thrust into it as he battened on her
areola, sucked hard and fast, and he could have sworn she
did, indeed, come, as her muscles locked, and her hand flexed
around his shaft.

It was beautiful to watch as she quivered. Justin seemed
to think so, too. Ecstasy burst through him, and he erupted
into her hand. He lowered his head to her shoulder.

"We're going to kill each other," he said.

"I can't think of a better way to go," she answered softly.

Caleb kissed her softly, followed by Justin.

"That was incredible," Justin murmured.

"And we have to go," Caleb said, reluctantly. "Don't
move, Ceili. If Jess slept through that, he needs the sleep."

It was still dark when they returned to kiss her goodbye.

"Be careful, both of you," she said. "Promise me."

"As much as I can," Caleb said, oddly touched, then
kissed her. "I promise."

She smiled and looked atJustin. "Promise me."

Leaning over her, he kissed her thoroughly. "I promise."

"See that you do," she said, and watched them leave, her
heart twisting just a little.

Her hands in Jesse's hair, she listened to them go before
closing her eyes and falling back asleep.

She woke to find her head against Jesse's strong broad
chest, his muscled arms curled around her. It felt wonderful.
She snuggled her cheek against him, and his arms tightened
around her.

"Morning," he said, softly, his voice still sleepy.

"It's a good morning," she said, cuddling into him.

"It definitely is," he said, his hands sliding down her back to pull her more closely against him. "Especially to wake up like this." He sighed. "But I'm starving. I missed dinner."

"Time to get up then?" she asked.

"I'm afraid so," he said, rolling her onto her back to take her mouth in a thorough kiss. "If I wasn't so hungry, I'd do more than this."

"We have all day, Jesse," she said, with a smile.

"We do, don't we? I'll meet you in the bathroom," he said.

She could imagine why, he still smelled of smoke. "Go, I'll be right there."

Quickly she stripped the bedlinens off, stuffed them in the laundry basket, and put a fresh set on. She used the crutches to get down to the bathroom herself. She did a quick rinse in the shower while he shaved.

She sighed, she loved watching him as much as she did Caleb and Justin. And he had a truly magnificent butt.

He helped her down the stairs.

They both poured bowls of cereal, and she noticed Ranger had a full bowl of dogfood and he was happily chowing down.

"I picked that up yesterday between runs," he said. "Let's take this down to the Cave. I'll carry the food while you make your way down."

Laughing, she said, "Well, that's an improvement over me being carried. All right."

The computer was fired up by the time she got down there. They ate while he scanned the weather and news on the big screen and she used the laptop to check her e-mail. They debated who was the greater idiot in politics and talked about a new version of a game coming out.

A new e-mail popped up on her computer screen.

"Jesse, would you mind taking me to the bank later?" she asked. "My replacement charge cards are in."

He hesitated for just the briefest second before he answered, but she noticed it.

"No, I don't mind," he said.

She set her bowl aside, frowning a little. She leaned on the arm of his chair for support so she could straddle him. "What's wrong, Jesse? Because something is."

Jesse took a breath, hoping he was right about what her answer to his question would be.

"Are you going to leave?"

The question made her heart twist. The thought of leaving him, them, of losing the pleasure of their presences, hurt more deeply than she expected.

"Do you want me to?"

Jesse wrapped his arms around her hips to pull her closer, looking into her pretty face. He thought of how much he enjoyed talking to her. The feel of her in his lap, beneath his hands, was wonderful. No, he didn't want to, he wanted to hold her, to fuck her as often and as much as possible, but he needed to know if she wanted the same.

"I asked first."

At the very least, Ceili owed him honesty. "I probably should, but I don't want to." And she couldn't make herself stop touching him, caressing his strong, broad muscular shoulders, running her hands over his taut pecs. In his own way, he felt wonderful.

"Good, because I don't want you to either." He slid his hands underneath the tee shirt she was wearing to slide them up her back. "I don't think any of us do. You're tough, smart, funny, you'll let us live out our wildest fantasies, and we've only just started. I want you to stick around, see where this goes."

"I do, too," she said.

He slid his hands down to her hips, pressed them against him, and rocked his own hips against hers to press his cock in the thin sweatpants against her. In one motion he stripped the tee shirt from her, caught her face in his hands, and kissed her slowly, deeply, and sweetly. Her sigh allowed his tongue to explore her mouth, to taste her, as her own tongue swirled around his, all the while rocking against her. He kissed and sucked the length of her throat, to bury his mouth in the curve of her throat, to suckle there as one hand curled around her ass, the other around her head to hold her tight against him.

She gasped, her hips riding him as he sucked hard on her throat, and he slid a couple fingers between the globes of her ass.

Lifting his head, Jesse admired his handiwork, the mark on her throat something he hadn't done in years, but he had wanted to brand her as his, theirs. His fingers continued to tease and tantalize her, one hand finding her nipple to roll and tug on it.

"Justin said you didn't seem to mind this," he said, his finger pressing against her anus.

She moaned a little, eyes widening at the pressure there, even as the fingers that had teased her breast slid down between them.

His sweatpants were in the way. He curled his arm around her waist to lift her enough so he could push them down, kick them away, before settling her on top of his thighs once more. The head of his cock slid across her damp folds, a lift of his hips pushed the head into her just enough to feel the size of him. His thumb found her clit, rubbed it gently.

On a soft moan, her back arched, the motion presenting her breasts to him. He devoured them, first one and then the other until she was writhing and moaning. Her damp pussy slid across the head of his cock, tantalizingly, as he sucked and suckled her breasts, nipped and scraped his teeth over her tender nipples. Reaching down into the pocket of the chair he found what he wanted. He squeezed the bottle, then found the waiting condom. He scooped her up, turned and deposited her where he had been, pushing the button that sent the back of the chair down. He spread her thighs and ravaged her clit, even as he slid the now lubricated, slender vibrating wand deep into her ass.

She arched with a surprised cry at the unusual invasion as he continued to suck, suckle, lick and lap at her clit, sheathing himself before he used both thumbs to expose her nub to his relentless oral assault. She bucked and quivered, crying out, as his tongue teased at her. Her hands locked on his wrists, clung there. He held her on the edge until he was so hard he couldn't stand not taking her. He sucked hard, and she shattered, crying his name even as he surged up her body to impale her on his throbbing, aching cock as deep as he could go. He could feel the vibrator in her ass teasing him as well. Her orgasm locked tight around him, gloved and stroked him. He loved this, loved her responsiveness, loved fucking her. Control vanished, he hammered into her relentlessly as he held her in place, pounding into her damp tight channel. She cried out as he took her harder and harder. He came with a shout, arching, driving his shaft into her. She took everything he gave her, her legs locked around his.

Looking up, ecstasy flooding her, all she could see was Jesse in all his rampant masculine glory, muscles locked, while his cock pulsed inside her, pouring his pleasure into her.

He collapsed over her, drawing her into his arms as he rolled her on top of him, to kiss her gently and sweetly.

Withdrawing the wand, he dropped it into the pocket of the chair as he pulled her into his lap and brought the chair upright again.

"Are you all right?"

She grinned a little shakily. "Mind blown. Poof." She mimicked it with her hands. Snuggling into him, she said, "Just give me a little time to get my brain working again."

Jesse didn't mind the snuggling bit at all.

"But I can't go to the bank in just a tee shirt," she said.

"There's a load of wash in the dryer," he said, "including the bra and panties Justin got you. He wanted to see you in them and wishes he had. He wondered if they fit."

"I'll let you be the judge of that. And I'd like to clean up the rest of the dishes from last night before we go anywhere."

As much as he regretted that she had to, he still enjoyed watching her get dressed. Just pulling things out of the dryer, she slid the panties on, and hooked the bra, bending forward to get her breasts settled.

"What do you think?" she asked, standing.

"I think my brother has good taste and they fit just fine."

He cupped one breast, rubbed his thumb over the nipple.

Blowing out a breath, he said, "I'd better stop, or I'll be bending you over the dryer."

With a grin, she leaned on the dryer and wiggled her butt at him, looking at him over her shoulder.

"If I hadn't just fucked us both nearly brainless, you'd be in trouble, love," he said. "So, get some pants on at least." He snagged a pair of his own and a tee and pulled them on.

Dressed, with the dishes in the dishwasher, they hit the road in his convertible Camaro, top up since Ranger was in the back seat, his ball in his mouth.

"We should do some grocery shopping when you're done at the bank. Not my favorite thing to do, but we just found this great cook," he gave Ceili a side-eye look.

"Did you now?" she said with a smile. "I might be able to help you there."

She ran her hand over the console. "How much power does this car have?"

"Enough," he said. "But given your track record, according to Caleb, I'm not letting you near it."

"Damn," she said, with feeling. "My reputation precedes me. Maybe we can see about getting a key for my car while we're out. I'm pretty sure my keys got lost in the fire, and the heat probably didn't do the electronic part of them much good even if I could find them."

She had downloaded a copy of her birth certificate, knew her passwords to get into her bank account, but while she could use her phone for some purchases having the card was still required for high ticket items and in some cases as an alternate ID.

"Do you need me inside?" Jesse asked.

She shook her head. "I shouldn't think so. It won't take that long. There's no reason both of us should be bored."

Maneuvering out of the car with crutches was helped by Jesse pushing her to her feet with a hand on her butt. Grinning, she gave him a look. Unrepentant, Jesse grinned back.

Swinging into the bank on her crutches, she asked to speak to the bank manager about picking up her duplicate cards.

"He's got someone with him right now, it'll only be a few minutes," the girl at the desk said.

She'd expected that.

Out of habit, she scanned the lobby, the line of people waiting for a teller to handle things an ATM couldn't, most texting or accessing the news or their email on their phones. A few were scanning information about Certificates of Deposit, IRAs and other investment opportunities. Others, like her, were waiting to speak to the manager or an investment counselor.

Something, though, was off. She hid a slight frown, pulling out her own cell.

First, there were too many younger men, not the usual ones with middle-aged spread or beer bellies. Several stood outside the less-traveled back exit to the bank – her escape of choice when cornered. One or two were inside and she could almost feel their tension. They were also more fit than most, but bulkier from shoulders to midsection than they should have been, given the muscles in their arms.

Alarm shivered through her.

Jesse was outside, so he didn't know. Ranger.

Trying to look bored, instead she used her phone to send a mayday to Caleb with the bank info, trying to appear calm. She needed to buy him time. She sent a request to Jesse to roll the window down for Ranger, just in case. Eyeing her phone, she knew the second Jesse got the message. Not knowing if he was seeing the same thing she did, she debated whether to send him the mayday, too, not knowing how he'd react.

The men inside the bank were slowly closing in on her.

She wandered seemingly idly toward a display near the entrance, looking out into the bright sunshine, putting a little distance between her and them. Outside, others were closing on the bank entrance…where Jesse and Ranger were.

Damn that was a lot of people just for her.

They were expecting some kind of a response and Jesse was in the crossfire. Cold fear spurted through her veins. She trusted him, trusted his training. She sent the mayday.

*****

Something was wrong, Jesse sensed it. As he looked around, he saw men converging apparently casually on the bank. Something about the way they moved was familiar, calculated. They were closing on their target with precision. One of them carried a duffle bag over their shoulder. Whatever was in it wasn't light. His alarm ratcheted up a few more notches. Ceili was in that bank. Robbery, or something else? Fear for her shot through him.

Jesse speed-dialed Caleb.

"Something's wrong, Caleb."

"I know, Jesse, Ceili texted a Mayday to me. We're already scrambling. Since she texted, she can't talk. Which means they're in the bank."

"She sent me a text asking me to roll the windows down for Ranger."

His phone vibrated. Ceili had sent a Mayday to him, too.

"I got the mayday, too, Caleb. We've got company, lots of company, bro. They're not taking any chances. They're armed for bear."

"Shit," Caleb said. "Jax, Bear and I were on a burglary call nearby, we're responding. I'm calling in another unit for backup."

Turning, Jesse saw Ceili near the doors into the bank. Her eyes were lowered. She turned her head a little to look behind her.

He understood. They were closing in on her and she knew it.

"It's going down, now," he said.

"On our way. You know what to do, Jesse. Stay alive. Both of you."

"I intend to," Jesse answered. Reaching into the glove compartment he pulled out his Glock, chambered a round. He didn't usually go armed, but since hearing Ceili's story, he had taken the precaution of packing.

He rolled the window back up again. "Down, Ranger, stay," he told the dog. With that many men firing, even Ranger's training wouldn't stand a chance.

The dog whined but obeyed, as Jesse got out of the car. He walked around it, leaned back against it, facing the bank as if waiting impatiently for someone. Which he was, to some extent. The gun was as hidden as he could keep it. His eyes were locked on the doors to the bank.

His heart was inside it. C'mon, Ceili. Come to me.

*****

Ceili knew the moment when they were almost too close and she bolted, heedless of pain in her ankle, crutches in hand. She hit the internal doors, burst through them, dropping the crutches behind her on the chance they might get in her pursuers' way or keep the doors from opening properly, and rammed through the outer doors.

More of the men were closing on the bank.

Jesse.

Fear for him shot through her. She saw him. Behind him… Another shooter, his gun pointing toward her, but Jesse was between.

"Don't brace yourself, Jesse! Get down!" She threw herself at him.

Jesse took the force of her weight as they fell, wrapping his arms tightly around her as a spray of automatic weapons fire went across where they'd just been standing. The windows of the car exploded. He rolled them as close to the front bumper as he could, searching for and finding the shooter.

"They've got vests on," Ceili said.

Center mass, even with a vest on, would hurt when a bullet hit it. Head shots, legs, whatever he could hit, would be more effective. Jesse nodded, braced the gun, and found and took out the shooter.

The time he'd spent on the range competing against his brothers had kept his marksmen's skills sharp. He wasn't the sniper Caleb had been and still was, but he could more than hold his own.

"Ceili," he said, "Caleb, Jax, and Bear are on their way. Don't acknowledge them."

The men were closing in

Ranger jumped through the shattered car windows. Running low he raced along the sidewalk, then leaped at a man trying to cut their exit off. The force of fifty pounds of dog, with a bite like a vice, was enough to throw the man's aim off.

"Go, Ceili, follow Ranger! I'll be right behind you."

"Don't get hurt," Ceili said. "I love you, Jesse. I can't lose you."

She already nearly had.

All around them people turned, innocent bystanders on the street, in the bank and shops, they could get hurt, too. Some were trying to figure out what was going on. Some, recognizing the sound took cover, fear and panic on some faces as people looked around.

It was her they wanted. So, it was her they'd get, and she'd pull the attention and fire away from Jesse.

She crouched in a low sprinters stance and then shot forward, running as hard and fast as she could, no longer aware of the pain in her ankle. It hurt, but she couldn't let it stop her.

The man Ranger had was trying to shoot the dog when Ceili ran past.

"Ranger, release," she shouted.

The shooter Ranger had had, his gun arm bloodied, turned toward Ceili. He grabbed at her, as she twisted away from him, not realizing the danger from Jesse. With people still on the street, there was too much of a risk of a stray shot. Jesse hit him with all the power his fear for Ceili gave him. The man turned to fight, but Jesse's second punch slammed the man's head against the wall behind him, and he dropped.

A gunshot. A car window shattered.

He turned. Ceili was still running, Ranger ahead of her, and the relief was enormous. She'd thrown her arms over and around her head, keeping it down even as Jax's big black SUV came around the corner and stopped.

Jesse followed Ceili at a run, Ceili drawing fire. The men moved to intercept her. She was running fast, but they were using the cars for cover. Brick dust blew from a wall ahead of her, trying to deter her or slow her down. Unsuccessfully.

Looking up, Ceili saw the men closing on her even as she saw Caleb, with two other men, exit an SUV. Her sharp, sure Caleb, in full SWAT mode. In all her life, she'd never been more grateful to see anyone. She almost ran to him, until she remembered what Jesse had said. It would become a firefight if they saw him. And there was Jesse, who would be caught between defending them both.

Several men suddenly stepped out in front of her. All were armed, their guns held at their sides out of sight of the bystanders around them, looking around in frightened bewilderment.

Ranger gathered himself, growling.

One of the men was already drawing his gun, his eyes on her dog. Her stomach twisted.

"No!" she said. "Ranger, stand down."

He looked at her, caught between his training and her command.

"Good choice," one of them said. "Mr. Janssen sends his greetings. Come quietly and no one will get hurt."

His gaze on her was steady, but there was something in them that turned her knees to water.

Almost everything went away as she stared up into his implacable expression, or the avidness beneath it. He was looking forward to whatever they had planned.

Ceili wouldn't let them see her fear. Nor would she betray Caleb and his men. From the corner of her eye she saw Jesse closing as well.

The leader turned to one of his men. "Kill the dog."

Her heart broke.

"Ranger, here," she said, and knelt to wrap her arms around him, looking up at the man defiantly. He'd have to shoot her first and something in his eyes told her Janssen had other plans in mind.

*****

All Caleb saw was Ceili, her golden red hair like a beacon, with Jesse behind her, covering her rear. She was sprinting all out, keeping low but running hard, Ranger clearing her path.

Then the men stepped in front of her, closed around her.

A glance to Jesse, and the four of them drew their weapons.

They were all close enough to hear the man's words.

Until the moment they drew, the men guarding the assailant's rear had only seen three men in plainclothes walking along the street. They froze as Caleb, Jax, and Bear centered their weapons on their heads.

"Police, drop your weapons," Caleb said, sharply.

For a minute, there was a breathless silence as the men debated fight, flight, or surrender.

The leader grabbed at Ceili to make her a hostage, but she was already backing quickly away.

Released, Ranger leaped, the threat to Ceili clear.

The man shouted as the dog's powerful jaws closed on his arm and hung on.

In resignation, with four drawn weapons facing them as lights and sirens closed, the men surrendered. They dropped their weapons and the man with the duffel let it fall.

Caleb and Jesse trained their guns on the suspects

"Stay where you are, Ceili," Caleb said. "Ceili, have Ranger stand down."

Ceili's eyes lifted to meet his and she nodded. "Ranger, release."

Seeing the look in her eyes, Caleb hated it, hated the pain and fear there. He wanted nothing more than to wrap her in his arms and keep her safe, but he couldn't. Not yet. By the look in Jesse's eyes, though, he wanted the same.

The dog let go, went to Ceili to sit and lean against her leg.

It killed Jesse to look at the tired, bleak expression on Ceili's face, but he had to wait. One wrong move, one of the men acting out of desperation and there was the chance everything would go south.

Jax and Bear moved in to search and secure the prisoners even as patrol officers came to back them up.

Showing his badge, Caleb identified himself, his fellow officers and brother.

The prisoners were secured and in custody.

In the next moment, Jesse had Ceili in his arms.

Feeling Jesse's strong arms around her, knowing he was safe and alive – this time – Ceili curled against him. Gratefully, she wrapped her arms around him, and laid her head against his chest hearing the steady beat of his heart. She breathed in the scent of him, and looked to strong, sure Caleb.

She wished she could hold him, too.

Then one of his men said, "Caleb."

He spread the opening in the duffel bag, to reveal the contents. They'd come prepared. Automatic weapons, grenades. Enough for a small war in some third world country.

Caleb looked at his brother, then to Jax and Bear, and to Ceili. She was just staring. Her eyes went to his in horror.

All this over a researcher. Janssen making a statement. He was also insane.

*****

The SWAT team debriefing back at the station had been pretty standard. An active shooter situation had been declared and announced. The proactive response of Caleb's team had been effective, with no major or obvious mistakes made or civilians endangered.

The detectives and others were still questioning Ceili in Interview One, though. She seemed calm. They'd let her keep Ranger with her and that helped. He was the true barometer of the mood she wouldn't show. The dog whined now and then. Once or twice, he'd growled low in his throat. He wasn't alone in that. Caleb, Jesse and Justin watched from observation. Some of the questions seemed harsh, accusatory.

All Caleb and Jesse wanted to do was be there with her, to take her home and keep her safe.

Jesse kept seeing the expression on the leader's face, the way he looked at Ceili.

Neither Caleb nor Jesse had been surprised to see Justin striding down the hall looking for them. Once word of an active shooting with multiple assailants had gone out, along with Jesse's involvement in it, and his station chief had called a backup paramedic in.

While they watched and listened, Justin had cleaned and patched up his twin's road rash from the fall to the pavement with Ceili.

Nor were they the only observers, Jeff and a few ranked officers were there, too.

"How's Ceili holding up?" Justin asked, but one look as Ceili's expressionless face and seeing her hand in Ranger's fur was all the answer he needed.

Jeff answered. "Pretty well, all things considered."

Looking at his brothers, seeing the same look mirrored in their eyes, Caleb shook his head, trying to keep his tone even. He hurt at just the idea, however much he knew it was true.

"She's going to run," he said quietly, for Jeff and his brothers' ears only.

Jeff shot a look at him. He hadn't heard that tone in Caleb's voice since his marriage had broken up. His brothers shared the same expression Caleb did.

"What? Why?"

"Because it's how she's stayed alive," Caleb answered. "It's her go-to response, the only thing she knows. For all the time she's been on the run, when no one believed her, no one understood how bad it was. People could have died today. Innocent bystanders. Someone she cares about could have been hurt. Jesse. To protect those others, and us, she'll disappear." As much as it pained him, he understood. "And because that's how she's wired. She can't fight them, but she can run. She can draw them off."

Frowning a little, Jeff said, "But she's believed here. We've seen it twice."

"We might need your help convincing her of that. The first few times it was just her in danger. Then it wasn't. This time was different. This time it's personal. Once before someone was hurt, but not badly. This time? An officer down the first time. Today civilians might have been hurt, innocent people, but more than that, Jesse, someone she cares deeply about, might have been killed. She also knows full well it's not over, and the next time it might be Justin, or me. Not for anything she did beyond trying to do the right thing. If Jesse had been hurt or killed…"

"Yeah," Jeff said. If it had gone wrong. Things happened no matter how prepared, how hard you tried to prevent it, those who faced it daily had to deal with that, try to keep it from happening.

"What she doesn't understand, or can't see, is that it's my choice," Jesse said, his voice tight. "It's what we all chose to do when we signed up to go overseas. What we choose to do when we came back."

"One thing," Caleb said, quietly, to Jeff alone, "I might ask you to do something for me, Jeff. If we think we're getting through, we might ask you to leave. Then you might want to go and clear the halls, because I don't think any of us are going to let her go easily." He almost smiled. "And Jesse, or Justin, or even me, one of us, will carry her out of here if we have to, and finish persuading her we mean what we say. First, though, we have to convince her."

Finally, the detectives and prosecutors declared themselves finished and released her. Once the release papers with her statement were signed, she would be free to go, they told her before they exited the room.

With nods to Jeff and Caleb, the ranked officers left.

Leaving observation, Caleb found Jax, Bear, some of team outside waiting.

"Jax, Bear, do me a favor? No one, but no one, goes into that observation room."

With a grin, a nod, and his usual half-assed salute, Jax said, "You got it, Caleb."

Caleb threw the door open and Ceili looked up.

One look at the expression in her eyes, and in two strides he was across the room, pulling her into his arms to hold her tightly, his hand buried in her hair to hold her head against his chest.

Jeff said, bluntly, "Caleb thinks you're going to run. Why? You have to know we'll do our damnedest to put a stop to this. Why would you run?"

Ceili started in shock, hearing it said so bluntly.

She looked up into Caleb's strong handsome face, his dark eyes so intent, and she saw something move in them. Her heart ached.

"I can't even do a simple errand without putting lives at risk. All those people in the bank, in the shops, any one of them could have been killed. And for what? Because someone wants me dead. They shot that cop to keep him from trying to stop them. They could have killed Jesse," she said, and the fear of that rushed through her again. She looked at Jeff, Justin, Caleb, and finally Jesse. She remembered seeing him standing there leaning against the car, his expression sure, determined, his strong muscled arms crossed. Ready to fight for her. And the man with the gun behind him. The piercing shot of fear for him at the thought he could be hurt. That she might have to watch him die… Her eyes stung as she looked up at Caleb, wanting him, them, to understand. "They could have killed him. And what happens next time? What if it's Justin, Caleb? Or you? Because of me, because of what I did, what I tried to do. And they just keep coming."

She was so tired, and so tired of running.

"I can't fight them, not on their terms."

Frowning, Jeff said, "You don't have to, that's our job. None of this is your fault. It's not because of you, Ceili, it's because of Janssen. You're one of the good guys, whether you know it or not. You don't deserve this. You've paid a hard price for trying to do the right thing."

Jesse went to her, drew her out of Caleb's arms and into his, held her close and tight. "Ceili, look at me. You have to understand it was my choice, it was my choice to help you, my choice to be with you, it's always been my choice. That's what I do. Firefighters go into a fire to save lives. Even if I didn't care about you so much, and I do, I would still have done it. Because that's who I am. Because of who you are, because you're still fighting. But I do care, very much. You said this morning you didn't want to leave."

"That's not fair, Jesse. I didn't, don't. You know that." Caeli looked up at him, into his blue-grey eyes. "They would have killed you. They could have."

Just the thought tore her up.

Holding her tightly, Jesse looked down in her eyes. They were too bright.

"It's who we are, Ceili, it's how we're made, all of us. This is what we do." Caleb put in, as Jesse surrendered her back to him. "It's why we served, it's why we chose to do what we do when we got out. I became a cop to protect, defend, and serve. To stand for people like you. You fought in your own way, tried and damn near succeeded to shut down a major drug pipeline. That it's you we're fighting for… It makes more of a difference than you know." He pulled her hard and tight against him, looking down at her.

Ceili reached up to touch his face, to look at the strength and determination in his eyes. She traced his jaw with her fingertips. She so wanted to believe. And she didn't want to lose him, Jesse or Justin.

Seeing her expression soften as it always did when she touched him was the first sign Caleb saw of her weakening.

With a look to Caleb, Justin took her to hold her close as well.

Justin said, "I became a medic and then a paramedic to save lives. We're the good guys, because someone has to be, someone has to do it. And, as Jeff said, you're one, too. You didn't have to do what you did, you didn't do it to be a hero, you did it because it needed to be done and you could do it," He looked into her pretty blue eyes. "On top of that, we never thought we'd find someone like you. Someone who cares so much, so openly and freely, as you do. That you let us do what we do to you…" He grinned. "That's icing on the cake."

For a moment all Ceili could do was gaze up at the warmth in his amber eyes. Lifting a hand, she traced his cheekbone with trembling fingers. She wanted to hope, she wanted to believe. She searched his eyes.

The expression on her face, the wonder in her eyes, told Justin everything he needed to know, even as it caught at him. He pulled her in close, his hand in her hair.

Looking at Jeff, Caleb said, "Thanks, Jeff, but I think you might want to leave now."

"And someday you might tell me why?"

"Or you might figure it out for yourself," Caleb said.

As the door closed behind the man, Caleb turned to Ceili and his brothers. "Jesse and Justin are right, Ceili. We kept trying to find someone like you and couldn't, we just didn't know it, weren't even sure it was possible. Then you just fell into our laps."

"Hey," Jesse said, in protest. "She fell into my lap, first."

Justin elbowed his brother, one arm firm around Ceili's waist. "Who was it who was supposed to share their toys?"

Desperately, Ceili tried not to laugh, and lost. It was too normal, too real. "Jesse, Justin, I told you, I am not your toy. So, don't you dare fight over me."

In that moment Caleb knew they'd won, now they just had to cement it. He hadn't taken the time to change into civilian clothes, so he had what he needed on him.

He said, keeping his tone deceptively mild. "Who says you're not our toy?" He looked at Jesse and Justin. Both started to grin.

"Caleb?" His eyes were gleaming wickedly. Ceili eyed him warily.

She was startled as he took her wrist and snapped a handcuff on it and then spun her around to bend her over the interview table. She felt his hips and more against her.

"Now that's a pretty picture," Jesse said. "You have such a nice ass, Ceili."

Pinning her wrists gently behind her, Caleb cuffed her wrists together behind her.

"Caleb!" She looked over her shoulder at him, her eyes wide. "You handcuffed me?!"

Reasonably, he said, grinning, "You are a flight risk." Sliding an arm around her waist, Caleb yanked her back against him tightly to whisper in her ear. "I think I warned you that I might do something like this once. I've been wanting to do it for a while."

Ceili remembered, a warm thrill rushing through her.

"Jesse?" Caleb said. "She's all yours."

His blue-gray eyes hot, Jesse slid an arm around her back, pulled her tight to kiss her hard and fast. Then he swept her up to toss her over his shoulder.

"Jesse! Put me down," she protested.

That was more like their Ceili.

"You do have a nice ass, Ceili. Oh, this is going to be fun," Justin said. "Just go with it, sweetheart."

Caleb opened the door, trying to smother a grin and destroy his reputation as a hard ass, although he wasn't trying too hard. Especially given what he was about to ask.

"Jax, Bear, you're about to not see anything."

Grinning, Jax said, his gaze going past Caleb to his brothers, and Ceili over Jesse's shoulder. "I don't see anything. What about you, Bear?"

"Not a thing," Bear said.

"You're all conspiring against me," Ceili said, almost mournfully. It would have been more convincing if she hadn't been smothering a smile.

"I intend to be against you as much as humanly possible," Justin said.

Taking one look as they stepped out the interview room, Bear shrugged out of his tactical jacket. He tossed it over Ceili. "You might need this, Caleb."

"Oh, this is just perfect," Ceili said, from within the muffling folds.

Justin said, "C'mon, Ranger."

The dog trotted obediently after.

# Chapter 10

Once they were in the car, Caleb returned Bear's jacket. Jax just grinned and gave his usual deliberately half-assed salute before Caleb slid behind the wheel, with Ranger in the passenger seat, firing the car up before putting it in gear. Concealed by the tinted windows, in the backseat Justin stripped Ceili's tee shirt over her head until it tangled with the handcuffs while Jesse unsnapped and unzipped her jeans. His hand slid inside them, beneath her panties.

Caleb glanced in the rearview mirror when she gasped.

"She needed to be distracted," Jesse said. She was hot and damp. "It seems to be working. I think Ceili's turned on."

Justin stroked his hands over her lace covered breast, her areola faintly pink beneath it, her nipples hardening. "It looks like that fits just fine. I want to see the rest."

With a grin, Jesse grasped the sides of her jeans and stripped them off. The rich scent of her arousal filled the air, as Ceili looked from one to the other.

He glanced at his brother. Nothing needed to be said, they knew each other too well. He said it anyway, for Ceili's benefit.

"Let's play."

Their hands wandered over Ceili the whole way back to the condominium, toying with and teasing her nipples, sliding within her panties to slip over her clit and into her pussy until she thought she'd lose her mind. Pleasure ran through her in waves.

Justin pulled one of the cups of her bra down to suck her areola and nipple into his mouth, his tongue sweeping over them, then he nibbled on her nipple. As he did, Jesse teased her clit, then plunged his fingers into her aching cleft to finger-fuck her.

Caleb glanced through the rear-view mirror now and then as they pleasured her until her areola was blushed to a deep pink, and her nipples were rigid against the bright blue lace. She quivered helplessly, her breath hitching as she writhed and wriggled. It was becoming hard to concentrate. Another part of him was rigid, twitching.

The garage door opened to let the car in then slid closed. Jesse reached in to pull Ceili out and toss her over his shoulder to carry her up to Caleb's bedroom.

Dressed in only the thin scraps of lace, her hands cuffed behind her, was incredibly erotic to watch as Jesse carried her up the stairs.

He tossed her onto the bed as Ceili watched each of them. Caleb flipped her over onto her belly and pulled her over his spread knees, her lace-clad bottom up.

"Justin, nice choice, these look wonderful on her fine ass," he said, caressing the firm globes.

"They do, don't they?" Justin agreed.

Hearing something in Caleb's voice, Ceili tried to look at them but couldn't. And she was so hot and aroused she couldn't think clearly.

"But she has to promise to behave and not run," Caleb said, and she could hear a touch of anticipation in his voice now.

"Caleb?" she asked.

"Tell me you won't run," he said. And brought his hand down hard on her ass.

The shock of it jolted a cry out of her even as his hand smoothed over her, and then his finger dipped beneath the lace to slide inside her.

She moaned.

"Promise," Caleb said, and his hand cracked against her ass again before his fingers slid beneath the lace to toy and tease her lower lips again. "Promise me you won't leave us."

Another smack, and then he toyed with her clit.

Each of them took their turn at spanking her while one or the other teased her clit or slid a finger or fingers into her, until her bottom was stinging and warm and she ached for more, ached to be filled.

"I promise, I promise," she whispered, gasping.

Justin slid her panties down her legs and then something pressed at the tight rosette of her ass.

"Oh!"

Lubricant warmed the entrance to her dark channel to a heated glow. Justin pushed the slender wand in a little, penetrating her, then worked it around inside her as she moaned softly. He slid it deeper as Caleb stroked her back.

Watching the silver wand slide into her had Caleb's cock twitching.

"Here, Justin, try this one." Jesse said. "One day one of us is going to take that pretty ass, Ceili." He stroked it.

"Or all of us," Caleb said.

Even through her erotic delirium she could hear the anticipation in their voices as Justin removed the one wand and pushed the new one against her. The warming lubricant made her intensely aware of what she felt pressing against her. The size of it as it breached her made her groan, pleasure and pain mixed as Justin worked it gently into her, twisting it, pushing deep and deeper still until it was seated inside her. They eased her to her knees at the end of the bed, then stepped back to admire their handiwork.

She trembled, the vibration of the thing and the state of her arousal rendering her helpless.

"God, you're beautiful, Ceili," Caleb said.

She was, her lovely blue eyes hazed with need, her areola blushed a deep pink, the muscles of her abdomen taut, her knees parted so they could see the curls between them. He tugged the cups of her bra down, so it held her breasts up a little higher. He caressed her, feeling her nipples hard against his palm.

Her brilliant eyes were on him.

Something else caught his attention.

"Oh look. Jesse, your work?"

Ceili's eyes went to Jesse, puzzled.

"Hmmmm," Jesse murmured, seeing her watch as he stripped his shirt off, then pushed his jeans off and stroked his cock. Her lips parted on a breath.

Caleb traced the mark on her throat, curled an arm around her tightly, then settled his mouth on the curve of throat and shoulder on the opposite side, and sucked hard.

The feel of Caleb's mouth on her throat, sucking so hard, was marvelous. Ceili turned her head to give him access.

Another warm mouth brushed over her breast to stop just above her heart to suck just as hard and as avidly. Justin.

Hands pressed her thighs further apart. Anticipation rushed through her.

Kneeling at the end of the bed, Jesse found Ceili at just the right height. Even better, trapped on her knees, she couldn't escape. He could drive her as crazy as he wanted, her body was his to play with. Slowly, he slid two fingers into her hot, damp pussy.

Ceili moaned softly, pleasure coursing through her. She trembled, her body tightened, released, tightened. Her hips pumped. She ached. Needed. Thumbs exposed her clit to lick and lap, suck and suckle. She whimpered.

"Please," she whispered, begging for something. She no longer knew what. Just more.

They stepped back as she quivered helplessly with need.

"Beautiful," Jesse said, his fingers brushing over her.

Her breath caught.

Ceili looked down. A neat red mark branded her breast. She knew two more matched it on each side of her throat. They had marked her. Claimed her as theirs.

Taking Jesse's place, Caleb settled between her thighs, exposed her clit for him to suck, to lick and tease. She cried out as he slid two fingers into her, then three, pumping deep and steady. She moaned, cried out, her body at his command as she writhed and her hips pumped.

His brothers each claimed a breast, to suck, suckle and nibble, bracing themselves and her on their arms.

"Please," she whimpered, and the wand inside increased speed. Soft cries escaped her as they eased her back on the bed, knees still bent, her thighs spread.

Weight settled next to her.

"Ceili," Jesse said.

She turned her head to find his cock there, a small pearl of precum at the tip, and licked it to taste the salty musky taste that was unique to Jesse. Hungrily, she took him deep into her mouth, and heard him groan. She hummed, and felt his body go tight. She found all the places that made him jump, felt his shaft pulse against her tongue, and took him as deep as she dared.

Justin took his turn at her pussy and clit as Caleb claimed her breast.

He whispered, "Oh, fuck me," at the sight of Ceili pleasuring his twin and licked and lapped at her clit until her body bucked and she cried out, coming as Jesse fucked her hot, sweet mouth.

Watching, Caleb saw when her pleasure took her, even as Jesse's cock drove between her pretty lips. His own shaft was rigid, but watching her as she came was incredible.

Ecstasy burst through her, and her body arched, trembling. All thought was gone, there was only them.

Her inadvertent quivering as Justin sucked her worked Jesse's cock. With a shout, Jesse came, his hot cum filling her as she took him, her throat working, and then he fell back, limp, his cum spurting over his lower abs.

Justin lost it, driving up to fuck sweet Ceili hard and deep, her body working him as well as her orgasm coursed through her. It was marvelous, and he was so hard, he couldn't pound into her hard enough, deep enough, but he tried. It was heaven. He drove harder, deeper, needing all of her. And ecstasy exploded through him.

Ceili looked up at him, feeling him pulse and throb inside her, then he arched, back bowing as he came, and she smiled.

The handcuffs were suddenly gone, and she wrapped her arms around Justin, holding him as he bowed his head against her shoulder. She stroked his hair and pressed her lips against his temple.

"Will you ride me, Ceili?" Caleb asked.

She turned her head to look at him. He stroked his rigid cock, and she saw something she couldn't define in his dark eyes, but it called to her.

"I'm good, Ceili," Justin murmured, pulling a pillow down.

She kissed Justin softly as Caleb removed the wand.

"I just want you," he said. "Just you."

"You've always had me, Caleb," she said, straddling him and settling slowly onto his shaft, rocking steadily. "From the first moment in the hospital when I teased you about calling me Miss Whelan and I saw how amused you were that I did it. And then that night when I had the nightmare. You were so beautiful to look at, so kind, and then so passionate."

His eyes were on her and they never left hers as she took him, every inch so deep inside her.

Caleb loved the feel of her hands on him, her warmth and dampness around him.

"You feel incredible." He rocked in time with her, thrusting up. "You were going to run."

Even though he understood her reasons, and unlike Alison Ceili hadn't wanted to leave, it still pained him.

"Not because I didn't care, Caleb, but because I cared too much. About you, about Jesse and Justin. The thought of losing any of you, no matter how, broke my heart. To get any of you killed? Just the thought…" Her eyes closed, suddenly too bright. "And if you had let me go, it would be proof you didn't care enough, but you didn't."

"Look at me, Ceili," he said.

Her eyes opened, focused on him as she rocked, and his cock moved inside her.

"And won't," Caleb said. He tapped Justin's mark on her breast over her heart.

Ceili felt the fingers of his other hand toy with her clit. He swelled inside her, his cock throbbing like another heart. "And I love the feel of you inside me."

Rolling on top of her he moved with more intent and Ceili watched his strong, handsome face as he pleasured himself with her, feeling when he came in slow steady pulses. She smiled.

Caleb sighed. So good, so sweet. He lowered his mouth to hers, and hers met his.

He collapsed over her, wrapped his arms around her, let his head settle to her shoulder. She stroked his hair.

"Love you, Caleb," she whispered.

He tightened his arms around her. Held her close. Held her safe.

Now to keep her that way.

# Chapter 11

Jeff was waiting to meet him as Caleb went to his locker to change. "Caleb, we have a problem. Follow me," he said.

A cold chill went over Caleb.

"A problem?" he said.

"One of the men your team apprehended flipped on Janssen and he's singing like the proverbial bird in exchange for a lighter sentence. Janssen has a hit list. As we've already discovered, he's using his ex-military and mercenaries in the US the same way he's used them overseas. He's been systematically but quietly eliminating anyone involved with the prosecution's case against him. And I mean anyone. LEO, prosecutors – as I found out when I reached out to the prosecutor in the Janssen case – journalists, and of course, witnesses. At the top of his list? Ceili Whelan."

"Why Ceili?" Caleb asked.

Finally, they might have answers to that question at least.

"Punishment, plain and simple. He wants to make an example of her. Because she was able to do what no one else had – put together enough evidence to force Janssen to flee the country, and she did it quietly, completely under the radar. Even his pet hacker missed it. They never saw it coming. That pissed Janssen off. Second, well, because she wouldn't die, either from sheer luck or smarts. And because she got away. Because she was able to do what few others could – drop her entire life and run. Most can't or won't. They have family, or family ties, careers. She didn't. No family, no significant other, and a job with easily transportable skills. Most of his successful assassinations were like her first two, seeming random acts of violence or car accidents. No one put two and two together. Except Ceili. So, she ran. She's been a thorn in his side ever since."

Jeff nodded to their resident geek, Leo. The man looked at him, then at Caleb.

"So, he's upped his game. It was bad enough before. Put it up, Leo," Jeff said.

It was an interrogation. Of one of the ones who'd surrendered. Not the leader, but his second in command as it were.

Midway through the video, Caleb was speed-dialing Justin. He was the only one at the condo besides Ceili, Jesse was on twelve-hour duty. After making up the time he'd taken after the shooting, Justin was off. He'd be asleep, but as a paramedic he was used to grabbing catnaps, waking at all hours to respond to a call.

"What are you going to do, Caleb?" Jeff asked.

Justin picked up, his voice rough from sleep, but alert and aware. And alarmed. He knew Caleb was on duty. He'd be calling for a reason. "Caleb? What's wrong?"

"Janssen's hired a sniper. He knows about us, if only who we are. How much he knows about us…? Is Ceili still working down in the Cave? If she's not, get her inside now. Don't hang up."

Swearing, Justin shouted, "Ceili? Ceili! Ranger!"

No answer. Caleb's blood ran cold. He was already turning for the weapons locker, Jeff on his heels.

He turned to Jeff. "Can you call Jesse and Justin's division chief? Get them cleared? I need Jesse's computer skills and a paramedic, just in case. Not to mention both are ex-military."

"On it," Jeff said, pulling out his cellphone.

The blessing of working with serviceman, no questions, just action. Especially in Jeff's case.

Over his own phone, Caleb heard Justin call, "Ceili, inside, now. Caleb wants you in the Cave, ASAP."

"Go get dressed, Justin," Caleb heard, then Ceili's voice. "Caleb, I'm heading down the stairs now. What's wrong?"

His heart twisted, part of him afraid of what she'd do when she told her, but he wouldn't lie to her either. Trust was a precious thing.

"Janssen's hired a sniper."

Ceili's breath caught, he could hear it. For a second, he leaned his head against the weapons locker. It was her choice, her decision.

"You have one, too." He could give her that. "Me."

"Stop," she said softly. "It's okay. I won't run, Caleb."

The relief that went through him gave him all the strength he needed, that and the picture in his mind of her direct blue eyes. "Good," he said, "because I'd have to go after you if you did."

He could hear the smile in her voice. "Then I might as well stay anyway."

"Just stay in the Cave, keep Justin there, too. Ranger, as well. I want you all waiting when I get there."

"What are you going to do?" Jeff asked.

"If they want a target, Ceili, my brothers and I will give them one. And I'll take out the sniper," Caleb said.

"I'll back you," Jeff said, "take what you need."

Caleb shook his head. "I'm going to take it out of jurisdiction, to decrease the chances of innocent bystanders. Besides, I have my own. I am going to borrow tactical armor, some ammunition, night-vision and thermal imaging, and radios."

"Going to the cabin, then?" Jeff said steadily. "Okay, I'll deal with the fallout, if any."

To Caleb's surprise and gratitude, the people from his team were leaning against his car. Jax and Bear, as usual, were sitting on the hood.

"Get off my car," he said almost automatically. The first time they had done it had been for grins and giggles just after he'd gotten it, after that they'd done it just to yank his chain.

This time was different.

"We heard," Jax said.

Marley, one of the few women to make it through SWAT training, handed him her body armor.

"I'm a bit bigger and taller that Ceili," she said, "but made for women, and it's state of the art. Try to bring it back without too much damage. That shit's expensive. Good luck."

"Thanks, Marley," he said, then held a hand up to the others as she left. "Don't even think about it, I can't ask you to do it."

"You're not," Jax said. "I've got time coming. I already put in for it. It seems a shame to waste it. And if you're going snipe hunting, you'll need help on the ground."

Snipe hunting. Well, that was one way to put it.

What Jax said, though, was only the truth, as much as Caleb hated to admit it. His brothers were good, but they weren't cops. Jax was a brother in blue. He had a cop's instinct.

He didn't like it, but he couldn't deny it. "Thanks, Jax."

Bear said, "I'll keep the team on the straight and narrow for when you get back."

His cell-phone rang. Jesse.

"What the hell's going on, Caleb?" Jesse said. "I was just declared off-duty at your request."

"Do you still have your drones?"

He heard the puzzlement in Jesse's voice. "They're up at the cabin."

"Good, that's where we're going, too. Janssen's hired himself a sniper. And, to judge by the past, he'll have backup. Meet me back at the condo."

He turned to Jax, told him what he needed as he packed the spare ammunition and Marley's vest in the gym bag in the trunk.

Jax turned for his monster of a truck.

*****

Rather than take the risk of being shot by mistake, Justin went to the only other room in the condo with no windows, the laundry room, and packed clothes for each of them. One item he held for moment, smiling at the memory.

He carried the bags down to the Cave, the irregular thumping puzzling until he saw Ceili throwing a ball against the walls for Ranger to keep the dog entertained and herself occupied. The dog raced after it happily, then tried to play keep away, but it was clear Ceili's heart wasn't in it.

"I packed a bag for you," Justin said and Ceili jumped. "Whoa, girl."

He pulled her into his arms, stroking her hair.

Ceili looked up at Justin, into his amber eyes. "Sorry, love."

"Nothing to be sorry for," he said, kissing her gently, rubbing her back. "You're scared. That's understandable. And you're hyperventilating."

She was, her breathing was too fast.

Taking a slower, deeper breath, Ceili held onto him tightly.

"You might want to check your bag to make sure I didn't miss anything."

Taking a deep slow deep breath, she said, "All right."

Grinning, Justin thought, *Wait for it.*

Ceili burst out laughing, holding up the thin tee shirt. "I don't think this will do much against snipers."

"But they'll sure envy us," he said, stepping close to tug her tee shirt out of her jeans.

Giving him a look, she said, "Justin."

He pulled her tee over her head. "You need a distraction and to get your breathing evened out."

"You just want fucked," she said.

"That, too," he agreed equably, unsnapping her jeans, sliding them over her hips. "Put the tee shirt on for me, sweet Ceili, I want to remember what you look like in it. Or better yet, what you feel like. I didn't get the chance, last time."

He unhooked her bra, pushed it off.

As she tugged the thin tee shirt on, he took advantage of that brief moment when she wasn't looking before he tugged her back to sit in his lap. He smiled when she gasped.

"You need a bit of a distraction," he said, his voice tight at the feel of her around him.

To Ceili's pleasant surprise, she felt Justin's cock fill her, and then his hands were on her, one brushing over her breasts, playing with the nipples, the other toying with her clit.

Only he heard the feet on the stairs, Ceili's head was back against his shoulder as his hips pumped and thrust into her, and hers rolled as soft sounds of pleasure escaped her.

That was the sight that greeted Caleb and Jesse, Ceili in Justin's lap, her thighs spread, her breasts swollen and nipples hard. Her eyes were closed, her mouth soft and rosy.

"Isn't she beautiful like this?" Justin asked, cupping her breasts. He could see their reflection in the TV screen. "She was hyperventilating."

Her eyes opened as Caleb dropped the bag, her eyes warmed and she smiled as she looked up at him, at them.

"She is," Caleb said.

Sniper or no, safe below ground, there was time enough for this. It might be the only time they'd have until this was over.

Caleb knelt between her thighs as she watched. He drew back the hood on her clit and lowered his mouth to it, sucking gently as his tongue flicked it.

She cried out.

"Yes, please Caleb, please."

All Jesse wanted was that soft mouth beneath his, to taste her. He devoured it. So good, her tongue finding his.

Justin groaned as she tightened around him, her inner muscles flexing around his cock.

Smiling, Caleb sucked her clit steadily, holding her in place as her hips tried to pump, her abs grew taut, and her back bowed.

He watched her splinter, watched her come apart as her orgasm took her. She cried out in ecstasy as Justin came, too, with a groan of pleasure. He loved being able to give her and his brother that.

Gathering her into his arms, he sat in the other chair and kissed her. "Thank you."

She cupped his cheek and kissed him back.

"It's too bad that either Janssen or the sniper can't see you like this," he said.

She laughed. "Funny, Justin said the same thing." She looked at Justin, who grinned.

"We are brothers, like minds and all that," he said, then sighed. "As much as I hate to say it, let's get this show on the road. We don't know how long or where the sniper is, so we're going to have to make him try on ground of our choosing."

Ceili took in a long, steadying breath.

"It'll be all right, love," he said. "And we'll be taking precautions. Let's get dressed and gear up. Jesse pack anything here you'll need. There's some stuff in the gun cabinet and storage I will."

Reluctantly, he stood, giving Ceili a quick hug as he ducked through the hidden door to the box room and the gun cabinet.

All of them wore vest under their tees, leaving the tails out so it wouldn't be obvious. It also covered the fact that all three were packing.

In the bag where the body armor was, he added his sniper rifle and a ghillie suit to the rest. His rifle didn't quite fit, but it would do.  -

"They know about us, if not about our relationship to Ceili, so let's play to expectations. A family vacation in the mountains with Ceili."

"I'll start carrying the bags out," Jesse said, gathering up his computer bag and a couple of the bags of clothing.

Ceili watched him go, her eyes worried. So did Justin, his mouth tight as he gathered the rest up and followed.

The trunk popped and Jesse dumped the clothing bags inside, keeping his computer bag with him

Slinging the bag with his gear over his shoulder and behind him, just as worried, Caleb nodded. This was one of the most dangerous times if a sniper was waiting for them somewhere here, they'd be out in the open, exposed.

"Let's go. Ceili as soon as we're close, get in the front seat. Ranger can go in the back seat with Jesse and Justin."

He and Justin kept close around Ceili as they neared the car.

Jesse walked around to the far side of the between anyone and Ceili. Nearly simultaneously they slid into the car, and he leaned across to open the door for Ranger and his brother.

"Ranger, road trip," he called, and the dog jumped into the car, followed by his brother after he slammed the trunk closed.

Both Justin and Caleb slid quickly into the car as Caleb fired it up and backed them out in a hurry, then drove at a safe pace through the residential streets.

"Why the cabin?" Ceili asked.

Caleb glanced at her, then back at the street. "It's too open in town, allowing too many lines of sight, with too many innocent bystanders. So many heat and light sources can also make it difficult to use either night-vision or thermal imaging effectively. Janssen can afford to hire as many people as he wants. With so few people, we need eyes in the sky, too. And some drones, like the ones Jesse uses, can be illegal to operate in the city.

The cabin is an old-style true log cabin, not stick built and wallboard. As big as those logs are, they'll stop almost any bullets. It's in mountains, on private property, and there's a lot of acreage. It's not hunting season, so there's few innocent bystanders in our part of the woods. In the mountains you have to pick and choose your vantage points, the hills, trees and whatnot force that."

She glanced at the speedometer. "You know, I've driven faster than this."

That surprised a laugh out of Caleb, breaking some of the tension. "Remember I've checked your record."

"A judge was really going to put you in jail for that?" Jesse said, amused.

"Three speeding tickets in six months with her driving record would try the patience of even the most forgiving of judges," Caleb pointed out.

"What's the fastest you've ever driven?" Jesse said.

"Caleb will handcuff me again," Ceili said, in a stage whisper, turning around in her seat. Although, to be honest, she almost wished he would. Another time, maybe.

"I'm not deaf, you know," Caleb said, entertained, especially by the impish look on her pretty face, and the sudden heat in her eyes.

She sucked on her teeth, and gestured one, one, four. "On a two lane and never crossed the double yellow.

"Damn girl," Jesse said, nearly reverently.

"I'm not blind either," Caleb said, shaking his head and chuckling. "And in any case, we want them to follow. Just not too close. We want to be able to get inside safely and get everyone in place before they have a chance to get set up."

The turnoff for the cabin was difficult to see and unmarked. Turning with a glance in the rearview, Caleb drove until Jax stepped out of cover.

Without saying anything Caleb got out of the car, walked around the back of it. He knew Ceili wasn't going to like this part, but this was the only way it could work.

"The cabin looks clear, Caleb. No sign that anyone has been in or around it for a while," Jax said, as Caleb pulled the bag with his gear in it out of the trunk. "I drew all the drapes and closed all the shutters. It's as safe as I can make it."

Caleb nodded, inserting the earpiece for the radios into his ear.

Now for the hard part. He opened the back door.

"Jesse, get those drones up as soon as you can," Caleb said. "Ranger?"

The dog hopped out the car and sniffed around happily, ears up.

Opening the passenger side door as Jax slid into the driver's seat Caleb crouched down by Ceili.

"Ceili," he began.

Ceili had been watching, putting what she knew and what she guessed he needed to do together. It terrified her, but she trusted Caleb, trusted his skill and training. Even so, she bit her lip.

"I know," she said and smiled crookedly. Her eyes were too bright. "I've seen the movies. I don't know what they got wrong, but I have to trust that you do." She paused, then blurted, "Caleb, you'll be alone out there."

"Not entirely," he said. "I'll have Ranger. You and I trust that dog's instincts. He'll alert me if anything is around that shouldn't be. For now, they'll only see a man walking in the woods with his dog."

"I hate this," she said.

"We'll find a way to stop it from happening, to catch and shut down Janssen, but to do that we have to keep you alive."

"Not at the price of your life, Caleb."

"I've survived a lot," he said.

"Even so, stay alive, Caleb. Promise me," she said, tracing the lines of his face. "I love you, Caleb."

She'd said it before, but looking into her face, her eyes, told Caleb how true it was. Everything he needed to know was there.

"And I love you," he said. And meant it. Time didn't matter, what mattered was the heart and soul. Ceili mattered. She cared, she fought, and kept fighting. Like he and his brothers.

And he loved her. So did they.

Her eyes shot up to his, and he heard her breath catch.

Sliding his hand into her hair, he kissed her, putting all of that in it. Then he had to go, time was running out.

"Ranger." He slung the bag over his shoulder, and then he was gone.

She looked at Jax. "Excuse me," she said to him softly, and slid over the back of the seat.

"We love you, too," Jesse said.

"Oh, Jesse, I know. I love you and Justin, too, and not one whit more or less than Caleb," she said. "Please know that. I can't lose any of you."

"We know that, sweetheart," Justin said.

Jesse pulled her into his arms, feeling her shoulders shake and his shirt grow damp.

Both he and Justin held her as she clung to them, just as worried for Caleb as she was.

*****

From the shelter and cover of his ghillie suit Caleb watched as the car pulled up outside the cabin, Ranger stretched out next to him. His hand was in the dog's fur.

He had a good position beneath a bush that gave him a clear view of the area around the cabin, and the bole of a large tree to cover him from one side. It was a little difficult wearing full gear, helmet and all, but better safe than sorry, and he'd promised Ceili.

Jax popped the trunk and they all got out snatching up their bags quickly before they went inside, especially Jax, because he looked nothing like Caleb. However, they needed the fourth heat signature. Ceili and his brothers paused for just a moment at the door to look out over the woods in the setting sunlight. Both Jesse and Justin had their arms tight around Ceili. He knew they weren't admiring the view, they were worried about him.

The sun gleamed on her hair. Sweet, strong Ceili. He loved her so much, wanted to look into those blue eyes and fuck her until none of them could move.

Even so, a part of him was saying *Get inside where you're all safe*. Then the door shut behind them.

His helmet mounted thermal imagining wasn't picking anything up. It could be days before anything happened. Nor was there a guarantee they'd been followed. He hadn't spotted a tail. That didn't mean there wasn't one. If there wasn't, Janssen's people would have to search for them. And Janssen had money enough for drones of his own. Nor would he worry about the legality of using some of them. Caleb was prepared for all of that, it wouldn't have been the first time he'd lay in wait for days until he had a good shot at his target.

He'd sent Jax ahead of them as a scout, to all appearances a caretaker closing up a house. Instead Jax had scoped out the territory. Having been up here for guys nights post-Alison or borrowing the place for a weekend away with his wife and/or kids, Jax knew the layout pretty well.

Then he felt Ranger go still, a low vibration in the dog's chest warning Caleb he had company.

Better to be prepared with good intel. In the service, a team would have ascertained the location of the quarry. A highly trained sniper would do the same thing.

The position Caleb held was a prime vantage point, which was the reason he'd chosen it.

If nothing was in front of him, whoever or whatever was behind him.

Caleb went still listening for the small sounds that might betray a hunter or hunters.

He debated his response. Take them down or take them out? When all was said and done, he was now a cop, even if he was outside his jurisdiction. If, like the others, this man or men was ex-military, then he wouldn't make it easy to apprehend him, and then what? He couldn't guard him, couldn't keep him silent. Shooting the man would draw attention, make the enemy aware that someone else was out here. And then the hunt for him would be on, which would divide their forces but also his attention, taking him out of the equation. If he killed the other, it would be hand to hand, a risk in itself, unless he could find something else to distract him.

He looked at Ranger, then looked over his shoulder with the thermal imagining scope. Someone moved at the edge of his vision.

Eeling out of the ghillie suit, Caleb took a quick look around for any others, a backup or partner, then slid out from beneath both the suit and the concealing bush.

"Find, Ranger," he said quietly.

The dog crouched low, then raced nearly silently beneath the trees and through the grass and leaves. Caleb followed, scanning around them for this man's possible partner. It was a gamble that someone was watching the man, but a small one. With luck, this was a scout.

Ranger stopped, quivering. Waiting for instruction.

The man was wearing military camouflage, standing in the partial cover of a tree, studying the cabin through thermal imaging binoculars, the two vehicles in front of it parked just far enough apart that someone could take cover between them, or to break up an all-out assault. Either Jax's or his brothers doing. The man had a gun in a holster on his hip, an M5 in a sling over his shoulder at his back. He was wearing body armor, but he'd left the helmet off to hear better.

Caleb crouched next to the dog.

"Get him, Ranger."

In a fast, nearly silent rush, the dog raced forward and leaped, his powerful jaws closing on the other's wrist. The binoculars dropped. Caleb move fast and nearly as quietly behind him. The man was trying to unholster his weapon. Clapping a hand over the man's mouth to keep him from shouting an alarm into his radio, Caleb put the man in a choke hold. The other fought hard, but Caleb was relentless. His brothers, Ceili, and Jax were down there.

"Down, Ranger," the dog released the man, and so did Caleb, lowering him to the ground, cuffing the man's wrists behind him around a small tree. The man's own balaclava served as a gag, his belt – sans weapons – bound his ankles. He'd be another heat signature if it came to that, easy to mistake as Caleb himself, he hoped.

"Good dog, Ranger," he said, and they walked back to his position, Caleb staying low.

*****

With Ceili and Justin's help Jesse hooked up fresh batteries in all the drones, and had his laptop fired up to display. Opening the door just wide enough he slid two out on a cookie tray, and then sent them on a pattern to slow scan. He had a program that controlled them, so he let it run, images flowing across a window on his computer screen, a third drone he used to scan their surroundings. Another followed, on seek and find, with thermal imaging.

"Why don't you show us all what you're doing, Jesse," Ceili said. "Four sets of eyes are better than one."

Jesse pointed at the screen, "Caleb is here."

"What's that?" Justin asked, pointing.

"Shit. Another drone." Jesse said. "Larger than my little ones."

"Guys?" Ceili point at the screen.

Thermal imaging from one showed that a figure had crawled up out of cover and was stretched out. He wasn't alone. As darkness fell, more figures appeared.

"Caleb," Jesse said quietly into the microphone. "We've got company, lots of it. Judging by the position, it's a good chance the sniper just appeared to your east. He was hiding behind the ridge. You're exposed."

Ceili's heart was in her throat, Justin pulled her close, but his eyes, like hers, were on the screen. Jesse's face was intent, but his shoulders betrayed his tension.

One of the windows on the laptop screen went blank.

"We lost a drone."

"Lights," Jax said, and killed the ones inside.

Jesse glanced at the screen. What he saw was enough. He looked at his brother and Jax.

He turned to Ceili, handed her the earpiece and mic. As frightened as she had to be, she nodded, her face set and resolute.

The only light in the room was the soft glow of the laptop screen. The only thing to be seen was Ceili.

"Love you," he said.

Ceili looked up at him, at his blue-gray eyes, then to Justin's amber eyes. She was terrified for them.

"I love you, too."

Taking her face in his hands, Jesse kissed her hard and fiercely, then released her so his brother could do the same.

Jesse drew his Glock, chambered a round.

Joining Justin, they took up position – Justin at Jesse's back.

A handgun appeared next to the laptop.

Ceili looked up.

Jax said, "Know how to use that?"

"The basics."

"Cover us."

She nodded.

Jax took up his position on the opposite side of the door, out of the line of sight through the shuttered windows. The shutters were their weakest points, wooden but thinner than the thick log walls.

*****

Rolling, Caleb put the tree between him and the sniper, even as he heard a bullet whiffle through the bushes to hit side of the tree where he and Ranger had just been. Settled on the other side, he sighted down his thermal imagining scope, searching for the sniper.

Took a slow breath, let it out, and fired.

He rolled behind the tree. Waited for return fire. Nothing.

That didn't mean there wasn't another shooter, and, as much as he wanted to be down there with his brothers and Ceili he would do them more good up here.

A soft familiar voice whispered through the microphone. Just the sound of Ceili's voice heartened him.

"Caleb," Ceili said, "We have company."

He nodded to himself, seeing multiple heat signatures.

So, the man behind him had been a scout. They had to be wondering what had happened to him and they'd be looking. With luck, they'd think the bound and gagged man was himself and not theirs. Caleb touched Ranger. He'd trust the dog's instincts over gadgets. And he didn't have eyes in the back of his head. But he had Ranger.

"Guard, Ranger."

The dog came more alert, ears up.

If she was on the radio, then Jesse, Justin, and Jax were taking position.

Night was settling.

The dusk to dawn came on, its harsh white light illuminating the yard. A spray of gunfire killed it. It also gave him a target. He pulled the trigger.

"Got 'im," Caleb said.

Ranger growled low.

Caleb rolled, drawing his sidearm. "Get 'em, Ranger."

At least two that he could see. Ranger had one – his target swearing as he tried to shake the dog off. The other man started to turn to help his partner. Caleb opened fire on him and kept firing as he sprinted behind the dog. Head shots. No use spending rounds on armor. As the bullets hitting his own proved. He lowered his shoulder and slammed into the man. They went down, but Caleb had his shot, and pulled the trigger. The man went limp beneath him, and Caleb rolled onto his back, firing up, hopefully beneath the helmet as the other man tried to bring his gun to bear on the growling, snarling animal. Ranger released, dancing around, darting in.

Caleb charged as the man tried to steady his gun.

*****

A sharp crash had all their attention. They all jumped and turned to look, Jesse's blood went cold at the thought that a sniper bullet might have gotten past him.

Ceili.

"Jesus, Ceili," Justin said, "Warn a guy when you're going to do that."

All of Jesse's computer equipment was arranged around her on the floor, the table now on its side, diffusing the betraying glow of the laptop now perched in her lap.

Her eyes when she looked up at Jesse and Justin were haunted.

"Get down," Ceili said, covering the mic. She didn't want to distract Caleb, who already had his hands full. He'd hear soon enough. "Things are about to get very ugly."

They all hit the floor as bullets hammered the cabin. Bullet holes peppered the shutters, but the thick wooden logs held. The chinking, although the logs were tight, didn't do as well. The thick wood front door held pretty well, only a few bullets getting through.

Caleb had just finished the second man and let the body drop when he heard the gunfire. He was already running for his rifle, diving for it as he saw the wood chips flying from the cabin walls.

"Sit, stay, guard," he said to the dog, pointing at the back of the tree. He wouldn't get Ceili's dog killed.

He sighted down the rifle as they slammed the ram against the front door. The door wouldn't hold out against that for long.

Keeping his breathing and his head focused Caleb pulled the trigger. One of the men holding the ram fell.

Around him some of his compatriots turned to provide cover, but the darkness covered him. He had the scope. Firing steadily, he tried to keep the door clear.

One, though, gave it a good solid kick and they were in. He had to trust to his brothers and Jax.

*****

Ceili saw them come in, saw them scan the room, their eyes settling on Jesse and Justin, both of whom were already firing. As was Jax. Their armor deflected some of it, as all three men tried for a good head shot.

Fear for them, all the years of running, turned to fury inside her.

"No, enough!" she shouted. "They're mine!"

Staying behind the table, she opened fire.

Her furious onslaught caught everyone by surprise. Justin took one look at her fierce expression, at her rage, even as tears streamed down her face. And nodded. She needed this, she needed to be able to fight back.

But she'd caught the attackers off guard, too.

He, Jesse, and Jax took advantage of it.

Outside there were shouts.

Inside it became a bloodbath. Everyone had taken hits in the body armor, and both Jesse and Jax had been clipped, but they were all alive.

Suddenly, silence.

Looking down at the laptop screen, Ceili couldn't see anyone around the cabin.

"Clear, I think," she said. Except for them, she couldn't see any heat signatures. Her voice was unsteady.

Holstering his gun, Justin went to Ceili, just to hold her. Jesse at his heels.

"I saw them aiming for you," she said, "and Jesse."

Jesse brushed the hair back from her face to press a kiss to her forehead.

A clatter by the door made them turn, the duffel bag hitting the floor as Caleb strode across the room to them, Ranger beside him. The dog bounded ahead.

Ceili. She, his brothers and Jax were all Caleb saw. Giving Jax a nod of thanks, he wrapped Ceili in his arms. Holding her tight he kissed her hard, devouring her mouth, before looking at his brothers.

With a grin, Caleb holding her for him, Justin took her sweet mouth, ravaged it. Jesse didn't give her any time to think, following his brother's leads, his mouth descending on her to kiss her brainless.

Successfully, it seemed, her blue eyes were dazed, her soft mouth a little swollen, but sweetly curved.

Turning to Jax, Caleb said, "Thanks, partner."

Jax nodded, leaning back against the kitchen counter he'd used as cover. On the opposite side of the house, the bookcase was toast.

None of it mattered to Caleb except Ceili, his brothers and Jax. "I'll have to call the Sheriff first, but let's pack up to go home while we wait."

They all knew what he meant, what they all wanted.

Gathering up their bags, they carried them out to the car, all of them stripping off their body armor and adding it to the gear bag.

"Caleb," Justin said, "you should have seen Ceili. Jax gave her a fully loaded weapon. Remind me never to piss her off.  The door crashed open and our girl opened fire."

"They were pointing guns at you!" she said indignantly, bringing out her own bag.

She started unfastening the armor.

Jesse tossed a ball for Ranger to chase, which the dog was happy to do. But he brought back the poor dead drone instead.

"She may not know how to shoot," Jax said, "but enough bullets in the right direction will get anyone's attention.

Rolling her eyes, Ceili shook her head, smiling.

Then Ranger stopped, eyes suddenly alert. Snarling, he raced across the yard and leaped.

"There's another shooter," Caleb shouted.

Four guns turned to open fire. Ceili ran for cover, intending to drop behind the slope above the river.

The sniper's bullet hit the body armor, but the impact of it still shocked her. The force of it hurt and turned her just enough. Another bullet hit her center mass, the impact driving the wind from her lungs and sent her staggering backward.

Jax's rifle was inside the door. Snatching it up, Caleb crouched, the gun against his shoulder and fired where he knew the sniper must be. On fully automatic he strafed the hillside, tossed the gun to Jax and followed Jesse and Ranger.

Throwing everything out of the trunk, Justin searched for his emergency bag.

*****

Pain exploded through her and then she was falling, tumbling helplessly down the slope. She struck the icy water of the fast-moving river. Jaws closed over her wrist, and then a strong, muscular arm wrapped around her, another closed around her, dragging her to the surface. She coughed and gasped. Jesse and Caleb.

The loose body armor was dragging at her, caught by the current, pulling her downstream.

Both men struggled to free her from it, stripping it off her to let it get washed downstream.

Ranger scrambled up the slope ahead of them, both men trying to get her up enough of the slope to get her out of the water.

"Are you all right?" they asked, almost simultaneously.

Seeing the concern in their eyes, relieved just to be alive and in their arms again she shifted her body experimentally.

"Do you practice that? Talking at the same time? And you're not even twins, only he is." She was having a problem taking a full breath.

Jesse almost snorted, the laugh and her comment caught him so off guard. "Funny thing, Justin and I have never been able to."

Letting his head drop to her shoulder, Caleb chuckled.

"Seriously, are you okay?'

"I think he dented me," she said, indignantly. "I can't take a deep breath."

For a moment they both laughed.

Shaking his head, Jesse said, "I'll go get Justin."

"Take Ranger. Don't say anything to anyone," Caleb said, "but Ceili's about to get dead."

It was her turn to give him a funny look. "Ummmm. Okay?"

So did Jesse. "What?"

Caleb grinned. "Trust me on this."

"Trust," Ceili said, "is not an issue."

"Okay," Jesse said. "C'mon, Ranger. Good boy. You found her. Good boy." He scratched the dog's ears.

"When that bullet hit you…" Caleb said. "That was a bad moment. I just want to hold you, make love to you, play with you, fuck you with Justin and Jesse, watch your body quiver and shake with the pleasure of what we do to you, to watch you shatter. I want breakfast with you in the morning, and to come home to you at night, you sandwiched between us, all of us sated and happy. You give that to us. I don't want to lose you."

Softly, Ceili said, "Caleb… I don't want to lose you, any of you, either."

Her fingers traced the line of his jaw, as she took a shaky breath.

Turning his head, he caught her hand, kissed the palm.

Justin slid down the slope carefully.

"What's this about Ceili being dead?"

"For a short time, Justin. To pull the dogs off her and give us time to find a way to stop Janssen once and for all."

# Chapter 12

The events at the cabin were all over the news. Ceili's purported death had brought Janssen's trial and the activities that had led up to and followed after it to the forefront. For the moment. If nothing else what had happened with her had shown how short the attention span of the news cycle could be. Once the sensationalism of it was past, it would fade. The days of the investigative journalist were passing. Janssen's activities had been exposed by the trial, Ceili had driven him out of the country but he continued to operate via both cell phone and laptop.

Efforts had been made in Congress to try to close the loopholes that allowed some of it, but those efforts had been unsuccessful.

"You know," Caleb said to the pretty woman with the cap of boy-cut black hair bouncing happily on his lap. "This would be easier if you'd stop doing that."

She grinned at him.

Now he was trying to work with the State Department to have Janssen investigated, so he was talking to one of the state department attorneys.

Her chocolate-colored eyes looked down at his hands as he toyed with her nipples. He missed sunrise colored hair and brilliant blue eyes intensely.

A voice answered on the other line, and he explained what he wanted and needed.

She wriggled in his lap.

Caleb bit back a groan. It was an effort to keep his voice steady.

He put the cell on speaker to leave his hands free. He tugged her tee shirt down to nip the tip of her breast.

Releasing it, he found her clit and toyed with it idly as he talked to the man. She arched and her eyes widened as she struggled not to gasp. With a grin, Caleb held a finger up to his lips for silence. The scent of her musk, her arousal made him even harder.

She gave him a look. He gave her a look back.

"If Ceili Whelan is dead, there's nothing we can do, Mr. Armitage," the man said.

At the moment, she was quivering in his lap, his stiffening cock going harder inside her as Justin slid a lubricated wand slowly inside her ass.

Jesse had installed a long mirror in the Cave, so they could all enjoy the view.

Her eyes went wide as it breached her.

It was the largest one they had ever used on her. He watched as Justin worked the vibrator in and out. The sound of its soft hum changing as he did it.

Justin kissed her shoulder just below the tattoo of Caleb's badge as he pushed it inside her until it was seated.

"The fact that this man had been dealing opioids and other drugs in this country isn't important? Or the fact that he's trying to do so again," Caleb said. "And he ordered the hit on her."

"Much of his business was quite legal," the man said. "And there is no proof of his involvement in her death. That's a matter for the local authorities."

This was what had frustrated the state attorney general.

"He's overseas, the local authorities can't touch him, but the State Department could ask for extradition."

"We need proof."

Ceili looked at him, unsurprised.

"You had proof."

"And he has a lot of money," Caleb said. "That he can use for campaign war chests."

"I can't speak to that."

"Thank you anyway," Caleb said, and disconnected.

It was about what he expected. It was why they were doing this themselves. Others, like several states' attorneys general had grown tired of banging their heads against the same brick walls. But they didn't have his, their Ceili.

He stroked the small tattoo of his badge on her throat where he had left a mark once before. It had been a surprise for him.

She was safe for the moment, but only until someone figured out she wasn't really dead, and he and his brothers wanted her back to herself. They had plans for her but right at the moment, he was in heaven as she gasped and writhed. Her body worked his cock, her internal muscles massaged his shaft as he toyed with her clit. The wand in her ass had to be making her crazy. It was certainly working on him, he could feel the vibration as Justin fucked her pretty ass with it. His eyes on the image of her lovely body quivering in the mirror, he licked her nipple, sucked on it hard and fast as she jolted.

"Jesse, Justin, you should feel this. She feels amazing."

Both his brothers were stroking their cocks in anticipation.

Jesse slid his arms beneath her to carry her to his gaming chair. He sat, his hands on her hips to ram her down on his throbbing, aching shaft, and she cried out with pleasure, her back arching as he toyed with her clit. As her internal muscles flexed around his cock, clenching it, massaging it, he cupped her breast to raise it to suck and suckle until the nipple was as hard and distended as the one Caleb had been playing with.

It had been nearly more than he could take to watch their sweet Ceili shudder and tremble on Caleb's cock, he's wanted to fuck some part of her, pussy or mouth, and he couldn't wait to take her lovely firm ass.

For now, though, he fucked her hard and deep as her body pleasured him until she was moaning and bucking.

That was the intention, to drive her crazy until they could all take her.

He looked to Justin, who smiled. Then to Caleb. Caleb grinned, lifting Ceili to carry her to Justin.

She whimpered in frustration, so close to coming. Caleb loved that sound, her need of them.

Caleb kissed her as he lowered her slowly on Justin's throbbing length. With Justin's help and her arms around his neck, he held for just a moment with just the head of Justin's cock inside her, and then both thrust her down hard onto Justin's shaft.

She cried out as Caleb stepped back to watch as Justin played with her, his legs spreading so they could see him fucking her. To feel her pulse around him.

If it wasn't for the dark hair and eyes, Caleb would have enjoyed it more, even so…

"Beautiful," he said. Because she was. He knelt between her thighs.

At the first touch of his tongue on her, her back arched. He took her up slowly as she writhed, gasped and pleaded, nearly uncontrollably.

Her hands stroked his hair, tightened as his mouth and tongue toyed with her.

Ceili thought she'd lose her mind, with the thick vibrating wand in her ass, Justin fucking her while holding her breasts for Jesse to suck on, and Caleb tormenting her clit. In the mirror she could see Justin's pleasure on his face and Caleb, his eyes closed as he tormented her so delightfully. Her eyes met Jesse's, and he sucked harder on her breast as he watched her watch him.

Her body was awash in pleasure, the muscles of her abdomen tightening.

But the contacts were a distraction, and she wanted to look at them with her own eyes. And she knew how much they loved looking into them. She tossed the things away.

When Caleb looked up it was into his, their, Ceili's warm blue eyes.

"Oh, love," he said. "Our blue-eyed girl is back, Jesse, Justin.

Justin whispered in her ear, "Welcome back, Ceili."

"And now we keep her back," Caleb said, fiercely.

She smiled radiantly as he lowered his head to her, sucking hard until she was bucking uncontrollably.

Sounds escaped her as his mouth, the wand in her ass, Justin in her pussy and Jesse sucking her nipples drove her slowly insane.

All thought vanished as they danced her on the edge of ecstasy.

She whimpered, moaned, pleaded, her body quivering nearly uncontrollably.

Caleb looked at his brothers. That was what they had been waiting for.

She gasped, cried out in need as his mouth on her clit disappeared.

Then Jesse pulled her to her hands and knees over him, his cock at her pussy.

He rammed it into her as the wand in Ceili's ass was gone, and she felt the broad head of a cock against her instead. She looked into the mirror to see Caleb behind her, his long lean body poised, his cock rigid as the head of it pressed against her.

That was the moment for which Caleb had been waiting, for her to see him mounting her, taking her pretty ass. He wanted to be the first to take her there. He was so hard, he wanted her, this, badly. But he also wanted her to know it, to see it, to feel every inch of him enter her, fill her.

He looked at Jesse as pushed the head of his shaft against that tight sphincter, felt it give. Even as he took her sweet ass, Jesse took her pussy. It was incredible to feel her so tight around him, to feel Jesse moving within her, too.

Ceili moaned at the sudden fullness in her ass, at the feel of Caleb's cock entering her. He banded one arm around her waist as he pushed it deeper. He was bigger than the wands, throbbing inside her, as was Jesse. As she watched in the mirror, Caleb thrust deeper into her ass and his hand curled around her breast, his fingers tugging at the nipple. Jesse's hips pumped and his mouth closed around her other breast. He sucked the whole tip of it into his mouth to suckle on it, pulling hard.

She couldn't think, only feel as Caleb's shaft drove slowly deeper into her ass as Jesse held her locked in place while he worked his cock around inside her, their pleasure visible on their faces.

Then Justin was on his knees in front of her, his throbbing shaft in hand.

"Suck me, sweetheart?"

On a gasp as Caleb thrust deeper, she whispered, "Oh, yes," as she licked the salty, musky pre-cum from the tip.

Justin shuddered, and it took everything he had not to ram his cock deep into her sweet, hot, wet mouth. But it was close, and then her mouth was around him. He groaned as Caleb and Jesse's thrusts drove her mouth over him.

Looking into the mirror, Caleb watched his cock disappear deeper inside her, Jesse beneath her, his shaft in her pussy as he sucked avidly at her breasts. Then Ceili took Justin's cock deep into her mouth. His eyes met Justin's, his brother's face was rapt, as transfixed as Caleb was on the image of all three of them fucking their sweet Ceili as her body quivered between them. Then Jesse's eyes met theirs. This was what they had wanted, to be able to do this, take their pleasure of her as they gave hers to her. But this, now, was her baptism with them.

All Ceili could feel was them, Caleb's cock going deeper in her ass, Jesse inside her pussy, and Justin throbbing in her mouth. She was drowning in the sensation of them taking her. So deep inside her, all of them. Her body was no longer hers, but theirs to command as pleasure shot through her. It raced through her veins to pool low in her belly. She writhed and trembled.

Every motion of their Ceili's sweet body drove them all mad, to watch her quiver and tremble between them in the mirror, Caleb's cock in her ass, Jesse's in her pussy, her mouth taking Justin deeper, was incredible.

Caleb drove his cock as deep inside her sweet ass as he dared, thrusting steadily, and harder. She moaned with each stroke. And pushed back, arching her back to give him more of her, Jesse more of her breasts, and taking Justin deeper into her mouth.

"Oh, God, Ceili, sweet Ceili," he groaned. The feel of her, the sight of her pleasure, theirs, was amazing.

All of them taking her had Ceili lost to anything but the sensation of Caleb swelling inside her ass, stretching her sweetly, as Jesse throbbed inside her. Then the vibrating wand touched her clit. Jesse. His own pleasure danced the wand over her maddeningly. Justin's hands clenched in her hair as he fucked her mouth. She was lost in them. All she wanted was to give them more, to take more of what they gave her.

Ceili's hips pumped Caleb, with Jesse's help, and the pure pleasure of fucking her sweet tight ass tried to obliterate his control. Not yet. She cried out around Justin's cock. Justin pulled free as Caleb drew her mouth to his, instead.

"Sweet Ceili."

He kissed her, hard and deep as another cock took her ass. Justin, the head of his shaft just breaching her, and then he thrust hard. She groaned, then moaned as Jesse touched the wand to her clit.

"Oh, God, she's so tight, so good," Justin murmured thrusting into her harder and harder. Like all of them, he wanted to take all of her. Everything. "More, Ceili, I need more of you."

He drove deeper into that sweet heavenly tightness, thrust harder, steadily, as she quivered, trembled, and moaned. His arm locked around her hips as he thrust, hard, and harder. It felt incredible. He struggled for control, pulled out.

Then Jesse rolled over, pulling his shaft from her pussy to seat the head against their Ceili's sweet, tight ass. "My turn." He'd wanted this for so long. He was going to savor it, all of it. He felt himself breach her, his legs spread hers so she would take him deeper and his brothers could see. He rolled over, so she would sink down onto him. And then he drove up into her, slowly, feeling every tight inch around his cock.

"Ceili," he groaned. "You feel

Ceili wailed with pleasure, touched by a little pain that vanished as Caleb claimed her clit, his tongue teasing it as his fingers thrust into her pussy to find her g-spot, and Justin sucked hard on her nipples.

Then all she could feel was the pleasure of what they did to her, as Jesse filled her more and more deeply, Justin's mouth on her breast and Caleb's tongue and mouth on her clit. She surrendered completely to them, trembling and quivering, heat washing through her with the glory of their touch, their taking of her. She was so close to coming again.

It would be now, Caleb knew. "Love you, sweet Ceili."

He surged up her body, to take her pussy as Jesse took her ass. Her body welcomed him, gloved him, stroked him. It was pure heaven.

Caleb wanted this, wanted her, for him, for them. So did his brothers.

He touched the wand to her clit, to feel her come around him. Her body arched as her internal muscles tightened around him, pulsing as she cried out. Ecstasy, hers first, destroyed his control and he came. He erupted inside her, his throbbing cock sending his cum jetting into her, filling her. Pure pleasure blinded him to anything but the feel of Ceili coming around him and his orgasm. His hands locked on her hips, cock throbbing, jetting into her, filling her. It seemed endless, brilliant, to feel himself empty into her with each thrust as she called his name.

All Ceili could see was Caleb, his long lean body arched over her, and his brothers. Every muscle in his body was locked as she came, and then he did.

Then Justin was there, his hand stroking an antiseptic wipe along his throbbing shaft. She had a moment to see him, his brilliant amber eyes glowing, his body taut, arched above her before his cock slammed into her ass.

Caleb slid up her body to take her mouth as his brother took her pussy.

Justin rammed into her, having only barely held himself back from coming in her ass. Now he set the wand against her clit to tease, to clench around his throbbing shaft, her pleasure driving his as she cried out helplessly. Ecstasy exploded through him, his back bowing as he emptied into her, his cock pulsing, jetting his hot cum inside her, and growled, "Ours. Yes!"

A wipe cleaned Jesse's aching cock and then Justin collapsed, spent, and Jesse thrust inside her as the wand drove her up again. Her body closed around him as she trembled and shook, Caleb holding her tight on one side, Justin on the other, both sucking hard on her breasts as she moaned, whimpered and quivered. She opened for them, her hands falling away helplessly, her thighs twitching as Jesse teased and tormented her clit for her pleasure and his.

The sight of her quivering in Caleb and Justin's arms, her body growing taut as her muscles worked him, was everything he wanted and needed to see. But more, to feel. And he did, feeling her come around his cock, her body tightening around him.

"Oh, God, Ceili," he groaned, as pleasure became ecstasy. He erupted inside her, his cum filling her, pumping into her sweet damp warmth as the muscles of her pussy stroked him tightly. His cock jetted his ecstasy into her, the pleasure so intense his body seemed to lock.

Even as Ceili's orgasm took her she was aware of Jesse's body rising above her, every muscle of it taut. Like each of them, all of them in their own way, they were beautiful to see when they came.

She felt his hot warmth fill her, joining that of his brothers, and smiled. Her thighs were damp with all their pleasure.

Never in her life had she ever dreamed of being taken so thoroughly or well. Or been so well-loved.

They all collapsed to the floor, Ranger coming over to sniff at them, finding the most inappropriate places to stick a wet doggie nose.

"Okay, okay," Caleb conceded, laughing. "Bed."

"So how do we do that?" Justin asked. "Get our Ceili back. Everything else we've tried hasn't worked. Except making her appear dead."

"The same way they did it the first time, but this time, everywhere," Caleb said.

"What?" Ceili said, surprised, lifting an eyebrow at him.

He grinned. "We unleash our research Queen. And not just here, in every country he has a presence, all at the same time. Just gather all the information in one place until we're ready to unleash it. Especially in those countries where he's had people killed, or with the help of those whose reputation he's tried to damage. Naming names. The politicians who owe him, the pharmaceutical companies who've supplied him."

Caleb watched her blue eyes kindle wickedly, her expressive mouth curve.

"A chance for me to finally be able to fight back," Ceili said, with fierce satisfaction. "On my terms, using my skills. I'm tired of being bullied, of running."

With a grin and a nod, Caleb said, "Exactly. He's been hiding out of sight. Let's drag him into the light."

Jesse said, "He's going to regret pissing you off. Go get 'im, Ceili."

"Damn straight I'll need your help, Jesse," she said, fiercely exultant.

"You got it." He looked almost as excited as she was. "This'll be fun."

"And what can we do?" Justin asked.

"What should have been done the first time," Caleb said. "We'll protect our Queen."

"Not just that. As I learned the first time, there are things that you as a paramedic know, Justin, and that Caleb as a cop knows, that I don't," Ceili said. "I'll need all your help."

Justin looked at the clock. "Oh hell, I'm on shift tonight."

# About the author

Award-winning author Valerie Douglas is a prolific writer and genre-crosser, much to the delight of her fans. She reads and writes classic fantasy, romance, suspense, and as V.J. Devereaux, erotic romance. Who knows what will pop up down the road!

And she's on the road - a Nomadic Writer facing challenging times with grace and optimism.

She's written 29 novels that reflect her eclectic tastes - high fantasy (the Author Shout Recommended Read) Coming Storm series, as well as Song of the Fairy Queen, historical fantasy - the Servant of the Gods series - mysteries, thrillers, westerns, and romantic suspense. She writes books for adults with rich character and plot-driven stories.

To get to know the author better, visit her Facebook page: https://www.facebook.com/Valerie.Douglas.Books

her web/blog page https://valeriedouglasauthor.com/

or follow her on Twitter https://twitter.com/ValerieDouglasA

*If you like this book, please leave a review.*

## Other Novels by Valerie Douglas

**The Coming Storm series:**
*The Coming Storm* Elon of Aerilann, Elven advisor to the High King of Men, helped negotiate the treaty between his people, Dwarves and men. He suddenly finds that fragile truce threatened from without by an unknown enemy and from within by old hatreds and prejudice. With the aid of his true-friend Colath, the wizard Jareth, and the Elven archer Jalila, he searches for the source of the threat.

Ailith, Heir to the Kingdom of Riverford, fights her own silent
battle. Her father has changed, but her quest to discover what
changed him puts her life and very soul in danger, leaving her only
one direction in which to turn. Elon.

To preserve the alliance, though, Elon will have to choose between
duty and his Elven honor...

*A Convocation of Kings* – sequel to The Coming Storm. A shadow
has fallen over the Kingdoms and once again Elon, Colath, Jareth
and Jalila are called to answer it.  One ally is lost, but another
returns while a terrible tragedy nearly costs them a third. Now a
member of the ruling Council, Elon of Aerilann and his
companions, Colath, Jareth and Jalila are forced to fight for the
Alliance they've given everything to preserve, even as a breath of
hope is offered...

*Not Magic Enough* - For Delae, a lonely landholder on the edge of
the Kingdoms, a frantic knock at the door on a stormy winter's
night brings more than a cry for help. After centuries of war Elves
have little contact with the race of men, but Dorovan can't bring
himself to ride past those so obviously in need. One small act, with
enormous consequences. Not Magic Enough is a tale of love and
honor, duty and determination.

*Setting Boundaries* - After centuries of war an uneasy peace has
finally been negotiated between Elves, Dwarves and Men, thanks
to Elon of Aerilann, Elven councilor to the High King of Men. One
final task yet remains, one final bone of contention - to set the
boundaries between their lands. For journeyman wizard Jareth it's
the opportunity of a lifetime. What he doesn't know is that the
journey will test him to his limits and forge a friendship that will
last for centuries.

*Song of the Fairy Queen* - It's said of Fairy that if you're in dire
need and you call their name they'll come. With his castle under
siege and young son in his arms, High King Oryan couldn't be in
more dire need. With only his High Marshal, Morgan, and a
handful of Morgan's men at his back, he has only one direction left
to run...up. And only one ally to whom he can turn.

Kyriay, the Queen of the Fairy.


**The Servant of the Gods series**

*Servant of the Gods* – A child of prophecy, she would bear many names. Born a peasant, she became a mercenary, was captured and enslaved, but rose to become a Priestess of Isis. As High Priestess she would face her greatest challenge yet and find a love that would last beyond time.

*Heart of the Gods* – When archaeologist Ky Farrar starts in search of the ancient Tomb, he awakens its lethal, and lovely, guardian. Both quickly discover Ky isn't the only one in search of the tomb and the danger to the world that lies within it. The key to which is the Heart of the Gods.

## Romance:

**The Millersburg Quartet**

*Irish Fling* – Ali was the smart one, but brains didn't stop her from crashing and burning. A desire to connect with her roots takes her to Ireland and a chance meeting with internet mogul Aidan O'Connell. Even brilliant Ali with her nearly photographic memory doesn't realize the danger lurking when she sees the wrong thing.

*Dirty Politics* – Returning to her hometown, practical Cam Kenyon discovers that teenage crush Noah Denton is running for D.A. When she discovers that his opponent is going to indulge in dirty politics, she throws her support to him, accidentally resurrecting an old enemy.

*Director's Cut* – When bad-boy director Jack Tyler comes to town to rediscover his passion with the local community theater group, teacher and theater geek Molly has to decide whether to take a chance on him. When his past catches up with him and he seems to be returning to his old bad habits, she has to decide whether to fight his demons alongside him.

*Two Up* – Sculptor and welder Jesse was always the wild child, her only real family her three friends. A chance meeting with novelist Mitch Donovan gives her a chance to make a new life. For Mitch meeting Jesse gives him new inspiration, but that inspiration comes at a terrifying price.

*Lucky Charm* – When private investigator Matt Morrison's best friend Bill is murdered, all evidence seems to point at his company, but Matt's every attempt at entry is thwarted. Violently. When pretty Ariel O'Donnell comes unexpectedly to his rescue, he resolves to keep her out of what is clearly a dangerous situation. Unfortunately, it seems Ariel is already involved and the forces set in motion by Bill's death are closing around her.

***Picture Perfect*** - Anne Sheridan, aka reclusive artist C. A. Calloway, finds herself in the middle of a high-stakes game of Monopoly, with dangerous consequences.

Michael Kelley, CEO of Kelley Hotels and Resorts, hadn't intended that when he'd offered to buy her property to build a new resort. That property was ideal for what he had in mind for a new resort. With so much money on the line, now he has to find a way to keep her safe...

A steamy, sultry thriller, Picture Perfect will set your pulse racing...

## As V. J. Devereaux

### *The Book of Demons series*
*Demon's Kiss*
*Demon's Embrace*

*Cherry's Jubilee*
*Special Delivery*

### *The Bound Series*
*Blood Bound*
*Magic Bound*

*Brothers in Blue and Red*
*Saving Maya*

www.ingramcontent.com/pod-product-compliance
Lightning Source LLC
Chambersburg PA
CBHW020921160726
47993CB00005B/2068